BAKER STREET BEAT

An Eclectic Collection Of Sherlockian Scribblings

Dan Andriacco

First edition published in 2011
© Copyright 2011
Dan Andriacco

The right of Dan Andriacco to be identified as the author of this work has been asserted by him in accordance with the Copyright, Designs and Patents Act 1998.

All rights reserved. No reproduction, copy or transmission of this publication may be made without express prior written permission. No paragraph of this publication may be reproduced, copied or transmitted except with express prior written permission or in accordance with the provisions of the Copyright Act 1956 (as amended). Any person who commits any unauthorised act in relation to this publication may be liable to criminal prosecution and civil claims for damage.

All characters appearing in this work are fictitious (apart from some real people in the plays). Any resemblance to real persons, living or dead, is purely coincidental. The opinions expressed herein are those of the authors and not of MX Publishing.

Paperback ISBN 978-1-908218-92-6
Mobipocket/Kindle ISBN 978-1-908218-93-3
ePub/iBook ISBN 978-1-908218-94-0

Published in the UK by MX Publishing
335 Princess Park Manor, Royal Drive,
London, N11 3GX
www.mxpublishing.com
Cover design by www.staunch.com

for my old friend

Stephen F. Winter

"the one fixed point"

Contents

RADIO DRAMAS

SOURCE MATERIALS

HOLMES, SWEET HOLMES

An Introduction in the form of a memoir

It's always rude to impose oneself on another without an introduction. Hence, this collection of Sherlockian scribblings begins with an introduction – of me and of the book. In it, I present the thoughts of a middle-aged man reflecting with pleasure on a life well read. A small portion of this essay is adapted from "The Enduring Mr. Sherlock Holmes," which appeared in the Classic Specialties catalog, Volume 4, No. 1, in 1991.

For me, it didn't start with Basil Rathbone.

I don't even remember when I first saw one of his Sherlock Holmes movies on late night television sometime in the 1960s. But I do remember the sense of disappointment. This Holmes didn't look at all like the Sidney Paget illustrations! And who was that buffoon going by the name of Watson? He wasn't at all the solid doctor of the Conan Doyle tales.

Sure, I watched the movies. I even kept a running list of the titles, awed by how many there were and wondering if I could ever see them all. But I had met Sherlock Holmes first in the world of books, and for me no cinematic version has ever quite measured up.

A boyhood friend named Ralph Eppensteiner performed the introduction. He lived in a house with bookcases on either side of the fireplace. And in those bookcases were 1920's era A.L. Burt Co. reprint editions of the *Adventures* and other Holmes books, including a collection called *Tales of Sherlock Holmes.* I picked up the *Adventures* and read: "To Sherlock Holmes, she is always *the* woman."

I had heard of Sherlock Holmes, of course – everybody had – but it was from Ralph that I learned the disturbing news that this Great Detective was a drug user. This shocked my mother, but it didn't stop me from playing Holmes and Watson with Ralph. I was the younger kid, about nine, and I didn't at all mind always being Watson. It was my job to bring along my wholly-imaginary revolver as we set off for our adventures in the woods behind Ralph's house. When I actually began to read the stories, I recognized many of the plots from having acted them out.

Like a generation or two of boys before me, the first volume in which I actually read Sherlock Holmes stories was *The Boys' Sherlock Holmes*, edited and introduced by Howard Haycraft. (Did girls ever read that book?) But the first Holmes book I owned was the inexpensive Whitman Classics edition of *The Adventures of Sherlock Holmes* with an illustration of "The Red-Headed League" on the cover – still my favorite Holmes short story. The collection was abridged in the sense that it didn't include all of the stories. But the stories were as God intended, none of this nonsense of adapting them for children.

Somewhere along life's journey, I lost my original copy of the Whitman book. It was like reclaiming a piece of my childhood when I replaced it years later for my modest Sherlockian library. I felt the same way when I found a *Boy's Sherlock Holmes* and many of the other books I had borrowed in my pre-teen and early teen years from the excellent Public Library of Cincinnati and Hamilton County – Vincent Starrett's *The Private Life of Sherlock Holmes* and

221B: Studies in Sherlock Holmes, William S. Baring-Gould's *Sherlock Holmes of Baker Street,* Edgar W. Smith's *Profile by Gaslight*, and others.

Long before I dreamed of being able to do that, though, I reached the point of affluence that allowed me to pay my parents $5.50 to order the one-volume Doubleday edition of *The Complete Sherlock Holmes.* I came home one day from the seventh grade to find a suspicious mound under a white tea-towel. Is it only in my memory that my mother removed the towel with a flourish reminiscent of Holmes in "The Naval Treaty"? The book had arrived! And it had more than just the stories. The Book (as my friend Steve Winter has always called it) also came with an introduction by a man named Christopher Morley that was magical; I read it and re-read it.

I still own that edition of the *Complete*, along with one that looks almost like it. The second is my wife's, bought while we were in high school or college. You can tell mine by the stain on the "A Note to the Reader" page – a faded chocolate-candy smudge that made me cry when it first happened. The dust jacket is tattered with wear and missing a chunk ripped off by one of our children in her infancy. (She knows who she is.) But I love it. I am of one mind with the respected member of the Catholic Church hierarchy who told me that his copy of the *Complete*, bought in 1950 when he was a seminarian, is one of his most treasured possessions.

With the *Complete* I discovered some of the later tales for the first time. (How I cried over "The Adventure of the Dying Detective," checking again and again to assure myself that it wasn't the true final problem!) Some of these stories came to be among my favorites, despite the lesser reputation of the post-*Return* Holmes. As soon as I read "His Last Bow" for the first time, I copied down the final exchange between Holmes and Watson and would read it with a dramatic flourish to other kids at school. Most of them were not impressed. But for me those words never lose their thrill, words I know by heart:

> "There's an east wind coming, Watson."
>
> "I think not Holmes. It is very warm."
>
> "Good old Watson! You are the one fixed point in a changing age. There's an east wind coming all the same, such a wind as never blew on England yet. It will be cold and bitter, Watson, and a good many of us may wither before its blast. But it's God's own wind nonetheless . . . "

Good old Watson, indeed! Somebody once said you could have Archie Goodwin stories without Nero Wolfe, but not Nero Wolfe stories without Archie. There are two Holmes stories without Watson, and he is certainly conspicuous by his absence.

For me, in fact, the most memorable passages in the Canon involve interchanges between Holmes and Watson, whether the context is a spectacular exhibit of ratiocination or a touching moment of revelation. I have always savored the last page of "Charles Augustus Milverton" ("Why, it might be a description of Watson!") for its delicious irony. And surely I am not the only one who cannot read this moving passage from "The Three Garridebs" without a lump in the throat:

> "You're not hurt, Watson? For God's sake, say that you are not hurt!"
>
> It was worth a wound – it was worth many wounds – to know the depth of loyalty and love which lay behind that cold mask. The clear, hard eyes were dimmed for a moment, and the firm lips were shaking. For the one and only time I caught a

glimpse of a great heart as well as a great brain. All my years of humble but single-minded service culminated in that moment of revelation.

"It's nothing, Holmes. It's a mere scratch."

As Holmes sheds his British reserve in near-panic, Watson retains his in order to reassure his friend.

The friendship between Holmes and Watson that resonated with me as a boy means even more to me now. Friendships formed in my own life have faded away, been interrupted by death – or, happily, mellowed with age into something even more precious than my first copy of the *Complete.*

It's no coincidence, I think, that many of my friends are friends of Mr. Sherlock Holmes as well. When we were students at the University of Cincinnati, my grade school friend Steve Winter and I teamed up with college friend Peggy Kreimer to have Sherlock Holmes parties. Since this took place in the 1970s, perhaps I should stipulate that the only drugs involved were those in the stories. Our merrymaking consisted of reading the stories aloud in all their glory, and on at least one occasion the Morley introduction as well. We appropriately called ourselves The Three Students, although sometimes others were invited.

I graduated from college into the world of journalism. As a reporter at the now-defunct *Cincinnati Post*, I wrote a column reviewing mysteries and mystery-related books from 1977 to 1982. Those were heady days for Sherlockiana, the immediately post-*Seven-Per-Cent Solution* era, when it almost seemed that one was liable to get hit by a falling pastiche at any corner. Some were readable and some were really bad, but none of them were the Real Thing. I kept them all, though. They became the basis of my library of a few hundred Holmes-related books, to which the current slim volume will be added.

Almost inevitably, I tried my hand at writing mysteries. I tried very hard, in fact, writing eleven unpublished mystery novels and several short stories. My greatest successes, in terms of publication or production, were articles, scripts or stories related to Sherlock Holmes. In this book are those that I liked best from those years – two essays, two short stories, and two radio dramas, all from the 1980s and 1990s, as well as this introduction and a new essay. Almost certainly none of them would ever have happened if I hadn't had the encouragement of Sherlockian friends.

Through a non-credit mystery fiction course which the late Rev. Lee J. Bennish, S.J., taught at Xavier University in the 1980s, I met Paul D. Herbert, BSI, founder and Official Secretary of The Tankerville Club. In short order I joined this Cincinnati scion of the Baker Street Irregulars, attending my first meeting in January 1981. I later pulled in Steve and Barb Winter as well. (I recall the shocked expression on Paul's face when I informed him that Steve had deliberately avoided reading some of the later Canonical tales so as to delay the pleasure. "Egad!" Paul exclaimed. "The man could die tonight!" The tragedy of dying without having consumed the entire Canon was not to be contemplated.)

Membership in the Tankerville Club – named for a club mentioned twice in the Canon – has waxed and waned, along with my own interest, over nearly three decades. Intriguing personalities have come and gone. For a variety of reasons there have been entire calendar years when I wasn't able to make a single one of the roughly quarterly meetings. But through it all, the Tankerville Club has been the one fixed point of my continuing connection to Sherlock Holmes. I'm also a founding member, with Dr. R.J. Senter, of The Scheming Minds of Sherlock Holmes for chess-playing Sherlockians. But the Tankerville Club actually has meetings.

What is it that impels grown men and women to put 221B on their license plates, collect obscure editions of books about an era long past, vacation at the Reichenbach Falls, wear deer stalker caps, argue about dates of events that (cynics say) never happened, and engage in other equally irrational behavior with like-minded lunatics in dozens of Holmes societies around the world?

In other words, how does one account for the enduring appeal of Mr. Sherlock Holmes, stretching from the nineteenth century now into the twenty-first?

In his own age – the late Victorian – the Great Detective must have resonated as a man of logic and reason at a time when science seemed to have all the answers, not just more questions. He battled speckled bands and hounds from hell with only the faithful Watson at his side and nearly always won.

Today, however, the world faces far more frightening monsters – the man-made creations of laboratories and bomb factories. What accounts for the continued popularity of Sherlock Holmes in these jaded and dangerous times?

Surely nostalgia for a time we never knew is part of it. The sleuth of Baker Street "provides the best picture ever set down of the focal point of the world at one of the high points of human history," Vincent Starrett wrote. Sherlock Holmes is "the spirit of a town and a time," in the apt words of William Bolitho, and we love him for that. But that is not the complete answer.

John McAleer, the late biographer of Nero Wolfe creator Rex Stout, pointed out that Holmes so far has enjoyed three pinnacles of popularity – each coinciding with a national or international crisis. The first was at his initial appearance, while Jack the Ripper still stalked the streets of

London. The second was in the 1930s, a time of great lawlessness in England and an approaching world war. The third – a particularly American renaissance – was in the late 1970s, on the heels of the Watergate scandal and a loss of faith in public institutions.

"In times of stress," McAleer wrote, "when [people] feel their property, their values and even their lives menaced or are disillusioned with those in whom they have put their trust, they find reassurance in rallying around a figure who is the embodiment of integrity and competency – someone who believes in law and order and can bring it to pass."

Could it be, then, that Holmes is hero and father figure in periods that sorely need both? He has his faults, but we know what they are. There's no chance that tomorrow's newspaper will contain some shocking revelation of a personal peccadillo – a fate to which flesh and blood heroes can fall prey even after their deaths. Although Holmes sometimes fails, he is always a reassuring presence. When he is around we feel that everything is all right. And, of course, Holmes always *is* around whenever we need him – never farther away than a wire to summon him and a train to get him here.

That is why for millions of us around the world, the game is still afoot. The game, in fact, never ends.

REICHENBACH PILGRIMAGE

Most Sherlockians who are fortunate enough to afford it eventually walk the streets of Baker Street for themselves. My wife, Ann, and I did that in 1997 as part of my first trip to Europe. We stood at the site of 221B Baker Street, visited the Sherlock Holmes Museum and were presented a business card by Mr. Sherlock Holmes himself. Away from Baker Street, we dined at the Sherlock Holmes Pub in the Northumberland Hotel and saw the tile walls with images of Sherlock Holmes in the Baker Street Station of the London Underground. Some years later, to my own surprise, I was privileged to make a less common excursion with old friends to the site of one of the most famous scenes in the entire Canon – the Reichenbach Falls. This memoir originally appeared in the Sherlockian Prescott's Press *in December 2008.*

Following the footsteps of Sherlock Holmes and Dr. Watson is not always easy, especially when it takes you off the printed page, out of the easy chair, and up the side of a mountain in Switzerland.

My Sherlockian friend Steve Winter and I, along with our supportive spouses, crossed the Atlantic to visit the Reichenbach Falls (after a six-day pizza and pasta prelude in Italy) on October 12 and 13, 2008. In booking our hotel and train reservations months before, we didn't realize that the Falls and the funicular taking visitors up the mountain would be shut down for the season starting on

October 5. Not least for that reason, our pilgrimage to the site of Holmes's fatal encounter with Professor Moriarty was an unforgettable adventure.

We arrived in early afternoon at Meiringen, the Swiss town at the foot of the Falls where Holmes and Watson had stayed. The clerk at our hotel, the beautiful and ultra-modern Victorian, assured us that the funicular and the Falls were both still running. Our excitement mounted. This was not what we had been told in an e-mail two weeks before by Rudolf Soltermann of EWR Energie AG / Reichenbachfall-Bahn. He had informed us, to our disappointment, "The cable car is closed from October 5th till spring and from mid October the Reichenbachfalls have no water." He did add the hopeful note, "In autumn, when it's not raining, it's still good for hiking."

Immediately after lunch at our hotel (our first order of business in town – hamburgers for four) we realized that we were right across the street from both the bronze statue of Sherlock Holmes smoking meditatively in a seated position and the Sherlock Holmes Museum. The statue was created by John Doubleday and erected in 1988. A plaque next to it, proclaiming SHERLOCK HOLMES HONORARY CITIZEN OF MEIRINGEN, informed us that the artwork included clues to all sixty Sherlock Holmes stories. Among the four of us, we identified . . . none. We couldn't even find the clues.

Barb Winter popped into the Sherlock Holmes Museum and came back with a report. "I have the news, and it's not good," she said. In fact, the Falls and the funicular were *not* running. Oddly, it had turned out that the man in charge of the funicular knew more about it than the clerk at our hotel.

No matter. Steve Winter, a man who habitually travels with a backpack and a Swiss army knife, wanted to hike the mountain up to the site of the non-running Falls immediately. It wasn't raining, and apparently Steve's energy levels were undiminished by an adventurous morning that had included the theft of a purse in Italy and the loss and recovery of a carry-on bag in Switzerland.

Barb further learned, however, that the Sherlock Holmes Museum would be closed the next day, a Monday. Since we were only going to be in Meiringen slightly more than 24 hours, we decided we would have to put off hiking for a day in order to visit the Museum.

No true Sherlockian would find it coincidental, still less inappropriate, that the museum is located in a former English church. This was, after all, a kind of shrine. The upstairs of the building is given over to art exhibitions, the bottom to Sherlockiana. The museum is delightful but rather small, highlighted by a painstaking reconstruction of the hallowed sitting room at 221 B Baker Street. It is behind glass, like the one at the Sherlock Holmes Pub in London, but claims to be the most authentic reproduction of the Baker Street lair in that everything is authentically Victorian, no reproductions. We bought a few Sherlockian souvenirs, but I was surprised how few were available. Barb suspected this was a factor of being at the end of the season.

The museum is owned by the adjacent Park du Sauvage Hotel, widely recognized – and proudly proclaimed by the hotel itself – to be the original of the Englischer Hof where Holmes and Watson stayed in "The Final Problem." In fact, the Park du Sauvage proclaims in English right in front:

> IN THIS HOTEL, CALLED BY SIR ARTHUR CONAN DOYLE THE
>
> ENGLISCHER HOF
>
> MR. SHERLOCK HOLMES AND DR. WATSON SPENT THE NIGHT OF 3RD/ 4TH MAY 1891.

> IT WAS FROM HERE THAT MR. HOLMES LEFT FOR THE FATAL ENCOUNTER AT THE REICHENBACH FALLS WITH PROFESSOR MORIARTY, THE NAPOLEON OF CRIME.

Clearly, Meiringen makes no mystery of the Holmes connection. This is a town where one can also buy Sherlock Holmes fondue and drink at a pub (or perhaps it's a private club) called simply "Sherlock" in bright red letters with a London street sign on the side of the building. Our attempt to dine at the Park du Sauvage, however, was stymied by a policy that their dining room is open for guests only, although there is a separate restaurant on the grounds. We had dinner that night instead at Das Hotel Sherlock Holmes, marked on all sides by a wonderful silhouette of the great man's head and an artistic lettering in which the "l" of "Hotel" is also the "l" of "Sherlock" in the line below. The meals, and the Swiss beer, were quite good. For dessert there was meringue, topped by whipped cream and ice cream. Meringue was invented at Meiringen, and they do it very well.

After dinner, we strolled and window shopped our way back toward our hotel. Swiss army knives apparently are widely available in Switzerland. Who knew? I also spotted some German-language Sherlock Holmes books in the window of a bookstore, one of which I was able to buy the next day at the last minute before boarding our train. We wound up inside the Park du Savauge, intending just to gawk. Instead, we bought more souvenirs, mostly for friends. The very nice clerk asked where we were from. "Cincinnati!" he exclaimed. "Every year I am going to Cincinnati!" He explained that he had a friend there who formerly lived on Clifton Avenue – the very street on which reside our friends the Senters, for whom we were buying a Sherlockian keychain! The world gets smaller all the time.

"Anybody can go to the Falls when it's running," Barb said the next day at breakfast. I took her point. It would be quite a distinction to travel several thousand miles to see where the Falls weren't. We were bracing ourselves for the task with a hearty breakfast. We had an impressive array of choices in whatever quantity we chose – cereals, yogurts, pastries, Nutella, cheese, salami, juice and varieties of coffee.

The plan after breakfast was for Steve and me to hike to the site of the Falls, with Barb and Ann accompanying us part of the way before they peeled off to concentrate on the arduous task of shopping. This was a prospect I faced with some misgivings – the hiking, I mean, although I had misgiving about the shopping, too. My concern was based in part on reading Sir Arthur Conan Doyle's autobiography, *Memories and Adventures.* In one of the most well known passages of that book, Sir Arthur wrote of determining to end the life of his hero in order to devote more time to what he mistakenly considered his more serious work:

> The idea was in my mind when I went with my wife for a short holiday in Switzerland, in the course of which we saw there the wonderful falls of Reichenbach, a terrible place and one that I thought would make a worthy tomb for poor Sherlock, even if I buried my banking account along with him. So there I laid him, fully determined that he should stay there – as indeed for some years he did.

The death and resurrection of Sherlock Holmes set a pattern followed in succeeding years by an astonishing number of heroic figures in popular culture. Father Brown, Lord Peter Wimsey, Nero Wolfe, and Superman all in some sense died or disappeared only to return to the living unscathed. In films, such disparate characters as the indestructible James Bond and the incompetent Inspector Clousseau survived their own funerals. The major difference in the case of the greatest of them all is that even his creator was surprised by the return of Sherlock Holmes.

And no wonder. No one who saw the Reichenbach at the peak of its might would readily imagine that a person – even Holmes! – could fall into that and re-emerge alive. Bear in mind, however, that the closest I have come to seeing the Reichenbach at the peak of its might was on DVD. Two weeks before our departure for Europe, I watched again the Jeremy Brett interpretation of "The Final Problem." I had two strong reactions to watching the fatal encounter of Holmes and Moriarty above the Falls: *That looks scary* was quickly followed by *Are we really going to go there?*

We really went there.

But on that fall morning, off in the distance from a point close to our hotel, the Falls looked more like the Reichenbach Trickle than the awesome force of nature described by Watson and showed to us by Granada Television. No matter. We set off with determination on the *Fussweg*, or footpath, well marked (at least at first) with signs bearing the universally recognized image of Sherlock Holmes. Along the way our wives fell back and Steve and I hiked on past cows, goats, and Swiss chalets with satellite dishes. Without the funicular "Zum Reichenbachfall," which marked "100 Jahre" in 1999, we had a delightful sense that we were walking more closely in the footsteps of Holmes and Watson than if we had taken the cable car much of the way up.

About two-thirds toward the top of the mountain, within site of the Falls, we unexpectedly came across yet another plaque. In English, followed by German and then French, it said:

> AT THIS FEARFUL PLACE,
> SHERLOCK HOLMES
> VANQUISHED PROFESSOR
> MORIARTY ON 4 MAY 1891

It had been erected in the 1990s by the Bimetallic Question of Montreal and the Reichenbach Irregulars of Switzerland, and not arbitrarily. The spot certainly fit the description of where Holmes and Moriarty tussled, just above a ledge now protected with a metal railing. Heights not being my favorite thing, it was to me indeed a "fearful place." Even the intrepid Steve told me later that he could imagine the fear and awe that one would have felt looking down into the chasm when the Falls were cascading over the jutting rocks at full force – especially in the days before funiculars, safety rails and well marked trails.

By this time, it was clear that the view from below had been deceiving. In October, virtually shut off by the diversion of water in order to provide hydroelectric power, the mighty Reichenbach is still a lot more than a trickle. In another context, with lower expectations, it would be considered a respectable waterfall. "The Falls, even now, are quite loud," I wrote in my travel diary as we stood on a bridge overlooking the great chasm and the cascading water. And their roar was the only sound to be heard in the stillness of nature that fall morning. Steve and I had seen no one else, except for a distant hiker that never came close to us. "This really was a pilgrimage for two," Steve said as we began our descent about two and a half hours after we had started up.

A pilgrimage it certainly was. For all the major world religions – Jewish, Christian, Muslim, Buddhist and Hindu – the pilgrimage is an ancient and meaningful practice for believers. It's easy for me to see why. Actually going to a sacred or important place, sometimes in the face of inconvenience or even difficulties, is much different from experiencing it second-hand. That's why people go to rock concerts, baseball games, political rallies and papal Masses when they could see the event much better on television or streaming video. It's why we made the somewhat convoluted trip to the Reichenbach Falls. And having been there, I will never read "The Final Problem" quite the same way again.

"YOU KNOW MY METHODS"

From the very beginning essayists and fiction writers have attempted to link Sherlock Holmes in various ways with his contemporaries, both fictional and real. Prominent among these was John Evelyn Thorndyke. Dr. Thorndyke was a purely scientific detective – not the first but one of the greatest and certainly the most famous of his day. And his day was a long one, stretching from The Red Thumb Mark *in 1907 to* The Unconscious Witness *in 1942, the year before the death of his creator, Dr. R. Austin Freeman. Dr. Thorndyke was both a doctor and a lawyer, an expert in more subjects than there are degrees, more handsome than any other detective in print, and wholly without eccentricities except perhaps for his penchant for Trichinopoly cheroots. He was 35 in his first case and 50 at his last – 35 years later. He apparently began his crime-solving career in 1896, what we might call the beginning of the late Holmesian era. Like Holmes, who was a scientific sleuth himself, Dr. Thorndyke has a narrator/sidekick who is a physician. Also like Holmes, he has a London address that is famous to his fans – No. 5A, King's Bench Walk, Inner Temple. So it was inevitable that scholars would speculate on the personal and professional relationship between Sherlock Holmes and Dr. John Thorndyke. In the following essay, I note the impact Holmes almost certainly had on Thorndyke in a particular landmark case, then extrapolate to a broader observation. It was written at the invitation of my late friend John McAleer, novelist and biographer, who among other protean activities edited a journal called* The Thorndyke File. *It is the most academic and least personal essay in this book.*

LESTRADE: "You are aware that no two thumb-marks are alike?"
HOLMES: "I have heard something of the kind."
"The Adventure of the Norwood Builder"

"A fingerprint is merely a fact – a very important and significant one, I admit – but still a fact which, like any other fact, requires to be weighed and measured with reference to its evidential value."
Dr. Thorndyke
The Red Thumb Mark

In a 1935 essay called "Meet Dr. Thorndyke," Dr. R. Austin Freeman wrote that his hero's methods "are rather different from those of the detectives of the Sherlock Holmes school. They are more technical and more specialized." Oh, really? A close reading of the renowned scientific detective's first case, *The Red Thumb Mark*, in comparison with the techniques of Holmes, indicates otherwise.

In the workaday world of law enforcement, fingerprints solve crimes and make cases. But in the annals of Great Detectives, they are almost invariably false clues. The way that Sherlock Holmes and Dr. Thorndyke each investigated a case involving faux thumb marks shows that Holmes was actually a role model for the later sleuth.

The red thumb mark in the 1907 Dr. Thorndyke adventure of that name is found in a safe owned by Mr. John Hornby, from which has been stolen an unopened package containing diamonds valued at thirty thousand pounds. The prosecutor states the case against Thorndyke's client, nephew Reuben Hornby, this way:

> "On the following morning, when he (John Hornby) unlocked the safe, he perceived with astonishment and dismay that the parcel of diamonds had vanished. The slip of paper, however, lay at the bottom of the safe, and on picking it up, Mr. Hornby perceived that it bore a smear of blood, and in addition, the distinct impression of a human thumb . . . I may tell you that, in effect, it has been made clear, beyond all doubt, that the thumb-print on that paper was the thumb-print of the prisoner, Reuben Hornby."

That is the entire case against said prisoner, which collapses when Thorndyke proves in court that the print was made by a stamp fabricated with the aid of a photographic process. It is astonishing to hear the counsel for the defense then say: "Of all forms of forgery, the forgery of a finger-print is the easiest and most secure, as you have seen in this court to-day." This comment, although published in 1907, was uttered in 1901 – the same year that Scotland Yard adopted the fingerprint identification system. No wonder Dr. Thorndyke speaks dismissively earlier in the book about what he called "the great finger-print obsession," the idea that a fingerprint affords evidence requiring no corroboration.

It seems that this great weapon in the Yard's crime-fighting arsenal was compromised from the start – or perhaps even before. In "The Adventure of the Norwood Builder," the 1903 telling of a story that took place in 1894 or 1895, Sherlock Holmes also exposes a forged thumb-print. This time the fakery is accomplished with wax. And it appears not as the centerpiece of a case, but as an afterthought. Holmes's client, John Hector MacFarlane, is halfway to the gallows for the presumed murder of Jonas Oldacre when Oldacre (alive and vindictive) plants MacFarlane's print at the scene of the "crime." That is Oldacre's downfall. "I knew that it had not been there the day before," Holmes later remarks of the thumb-print. Oldacre, he observes, "had not that supreme gift of the artist, the knowledge of when to stop."

Francis M. Currier, in "Holmes and Thorndyke: A Real Friendship," concludes that Thorndyke must have gotten the concept of the forged thumb-print from Holmes. That is reasonable, but Currier is too timid in drawing his inferences, as Holmes complained of Watson.

Consider the remarkable coincidences in the two criminal cases: In both of them a bloody thumb-print was involved (the left for Thorndyke, the right for Holmes). In both of them the detective champions a client who later turns out to be the victim of a frame-up via forged print. And in both of them the murderer is a jilted suitor! This is a grand example of Holmes's assertion in *The Valley of Fear* that "The old wheel turns, and the same spoke comes up. It's all been done before, and will be again."

This wasn't just a philosophical observation but a matter of great practical value to Holmes. In "The Red-Headed League," he notes, "As a rule, when I have heard some slight indication of the course of events, I am able to guide myself by the thousands of other similar cases which occur to my memory." Holmes does this throughout the Canon, repeatedly consulting his famous commonplace books. It is a *modus operandi* that dates back to his first published case, for he noted rather biblically in *A Study in Scarlet*, "There is nothing new under the sun. It has all been done before."

The resident of No. 5A, King's Bench Walk, Inner Temple, clearly paid similar attention to parallel cases, which is why he learned so much from Holmes's experience in the matter of the Norwood builder. But the broader and more important conclusion to be drawn is that this foremost medico-legal expert, the one-man CSI of his day, owed much of his overall method from the beginning of his career to the world's first consulting detective.

Thorndyke said in *The Red Thumb Mark* that he made it a rule "to proceed on the strictly classical lines of inductive inquiry – collect facts, make hypotheses, test them and seek for verification. And I always endeavor to keep an open mind." Save for the fact that he called what he did deduction instead of induction, Sherlock Holmes could have said that. Holmes did say, in "The Crooked Man" and elsewhere, "You know my methods, Watson." Dr. Thorndyke not only knew them, he applied them.

Later in *The Red Thumb Mark*, the Watson-like narrator Dr. Jervis tells his love interest, "Dr. Thorndyke is as close as an oyster. He treats me as he treats every one else – he listens attentively, observes closely, and says nothing." Later, he tells another character: "Thorndyke is a man who plays a single-handed game and no one knows what cards he holds until he lays them on the table."

Now, who does *that* sound like?

In his attempt to distinguish the methods of his protagonist from "those of the detectives of the Sherlock Holmes school," R. Austin Freeman went on to write that Dr. Thornkyke "is a medico-legal expert, and his methods are those of medico-legal science." The same could be said of Holmes, from his debut appearance in *A Study in Scarlet* to his last in "The Adventure of Shoscombe Old Place" and points between. Holmes is as at-home with beakers, test tubes and microscopes as with disguises and revolvers.

Recall Dr. Watson's unforgettable first encounter with young Sherlock Holmes in the chemical laboratory at St. Bart's:

> This was a lofty chamber, lined and littered with countless bottles. Broad, low tables were scattered about, which bristled with retorts, test-tubes, and little Bunsen lamps, with their blue flickering flames. There was only one student in the room, who was bending over a distant table absorbed in his work. At the sound of our steps he glanced round and sprang to his feet with a cry of pleasure. "I've found it! I've found it," he shouted to my companion, running towards us with a test-tube in his hand. "I have found a re-agent which is precipitated by hemoglobin, and by nothing else."

After being introduced to Watson ("You have been in Afghanistan, I perceive"), Holmes explains excitedly that "it is the most practical medical-legal discovery for years. Don't you see that it gives an infallible test for blood-stains?" He mentions five cases around the world, and alludes to another score, in which the Sherlock Holmes test would have been decisive.

Perhaps this is the very test that Holmes is performing at the beginning of "The Naval Treaty," which finds Holmes "clad in his dressing gown and working hard over a chemical investigation."

> "You come at a crisis, Watson," said he. "If this paper remains blue, all is well. If it turns red, it means a man's life." He dipped it into the test-tube and it flushed at once into a dull, dirty crimson. "Hum! I thought as much!" he cried.

Nowhere is it recorded that Dr. Thorndyke himself used the Sherlock Holmes test, but can there be any real doubt?

The test tube was not the only scientific weapon in Holmes's arson. His last published adventure, "The Adventure of Shoscombe Old Place," begins with the consulting detective straightening up from a low-powered microscope to look at Watson in triumph. "It is glue, Watson. Unquestionably it is glue." Thus is it established that a cap found beside a dead policeman likely belongs to the accused, a picture-frame maker who habitually handles glue.

The case at hand is one that Holmes has undertaken at the behest of his friend Merivale of the Yard. "Since I ran down that coiner by the zinc and copper filings in the seam of his cuff they have begun to realize the importance of the microscope," he tells Watson. (This is another mention of a case about which Watson does not provide a full account.)

It is true that Watson, the man of action, never gives us more than tantalizing glimpses of the medico-legal Holmes, preferring instead the perhaps more dramatic tales to the scientifically solved. Nevertheless, even these side notes to the sensational make it clear that Dr. Thorndyke, although a giant in his own right, stood on the shoulders of Sherlock Holmes.

WRITING THE HOLMES PASTICHE

The typical format of Tankerville Club meetings involves a social hour, an insanely difficult Sherlockian quiz created by our Official Secretary, and a discussion of a pre-selected story from the Canon. On rare occasions there is a special presentation. One such occasion was when I delivered the following presentation on the art of pastiche writing. I have only written one pastiche, but I have read dozens – most of them disappointing at best. Thus my thoughts on the subject were based on years of observation as to what works and what doesn't. I am deeply indebted to Paul Herbert, BSI, and to Jon L. Lellenberg, BSI, both of whom kindly read and corrected this print version of the presentation. It was first published in the May 1991 issue of the Sherlockian journal Wheelwrightings *under the title "The Art of the Pastiche."*

In 1911 an unemployed architect named Arthur Whitaker sent A. Conan Doyle an original Sherlock Holmes story and a suggestion – that Conan Doyle join him as co-author to get the tale published. Dr. Watson's generous literary agent ultimately sent back ten guineas for the plot idea (which he never used), but he urged Whitaker to try rewriting the story without Holmes. In essence, he was saying:

"Create your own characters!"

That's good advice for any writer with literary aspirations, then and now.

Because of its derivative nature the pastiche is understandably regarded as an inferior literary form. It is an imitation and can never be anything more. Imagine the ultimate pastiche: It reads exactly like the real thing. If read aloud it even *sounds* like the real thing. But it is not and can never *be* the real thing. After all, there's no pastiche like Holmes. And who among us – given the choice – would not prefer just one genuine new Sherlock Holmes story, however far from the best, to a whole Library of Congress full of pastiches?

The author of a pastiche must recreate, or in some cases re-envision, another writer's world instead of creating his or her own. That is craft, not art. The resulting work inevitably will be judged not on its own merits, but on how it stacks up against the original. And by this yardstick it must always fall short because it is, in fact, *not* the original.

Still, people write pastiches – especially about Sherlock Holmes. Why is this so?

Certainly a ready market is one reason. After Nicholas Meyer's *The Seven-Per-Cent Solution* hit the best-seller lists in 1974, a flood of Holmes pastiches were produced and published. Meyer had proved that new Holmes adventures could be not only popular but profitable. The flood was turned into a trickle and then dammed altogether for a while after the American rights to Sherlock Holmes retuned to the Conan Doyle family in 1981. To her great credit, Dame Jean Conan Doyle – the late author's last living child – insisted that pastiches be well written and true to the spirit of the original. (Whether those strictures were always successfully applied is, of course, a matter of subjective opinion.) Dame Jean never stopped disliking pastiches in principle, however, and by the early 1990s had stopped authorizing any new Holmes stories for commercial publication in the United States beyond a small number already in the pipeline. Today, with copyrights expired, Holmes belongs to anybody who wants to write about him. And sometimes it seems that almost everybody does.

Undoubtedly, genuine love of Sherlock Holmes and his world motivates many pastiche writers, whether they are turning out tales for commercial publication or for the enjoyment of the Sherlockian community. This is more than just the sincerest form of flattery, although it is that. It is as though the authors wish to ensure that Holmes and Watson will live forever by imagining new adventures and writing new stories about them.

For myself, I was drawn to add my contribution to the world oversupply of Sherlock Holmes pastiches by the hope of winning a contest, which I did. Along the way, I found another reason for writing pastiches: It is highly instructive. When you learn first-hand how difficult it is to write what you hope is a passable imitation, your wonder and appreciation at the original can only grow.

Based partly on that experience, as well as on decades of reading the Canon and both good and bad attempts to replicate it, I wish to offer here some helpful hints for writing the Holmes pastiche.

Let's start with the big picture. Mystery author and critic Julian Symons once observed that "Sherlock Holmes is mostly an attitude and a few lines of unforgettable dialogue." The comment may sound disparaging, and perhaps was meant to be, but it is no less true for that. Attitude and dialogue are major components of the Holmes mystique. It is that attitude that must be captured in a pastiche. The story should *read* and *feel* as though it came from the pen of Dr. Watson – but without actually lifting words right out of the Canon. Instead of repeating some version of the too-familiar, "When you have eliminated the impossible . . . ," for example, invent your own Sherlockian aphorism. You want the reader to think, "That sounds like Holmes, all right!"

In the parts that are not dialogue, strive for a Watsonian tone with the words you choose. From the title to the last word of the story, Watson is always heavily descriptive of people, buildings, even ambiance. He never leaves you wondering what the weather is like, for example.

If you are an American, remember that you are writing in a different language. Labour to colour your story with British spellings.

Martin Arbagi offers sound advice on emulating Dr. Watson's style: Don't be too archaic *or* too modern. And don't explain yourself too much – remember, you are writing in a Victorian style for a Victorian audience that doesn't need to be told that Price Albert is Queen Victoria's husband.

Period is a key element in the magic of Sherlock Holmes, so keep some key reference books handy to make sure you don't commit any anachronisms.

It goes without saying that the characters and the format should be the same as in the original. If it's not a first-person narrative by Watson featuring Holmes, then it isn't a Holmes pastiche. It might be a Holmes *story*, but not a *pastiche.* I haven't forgotten that four stories in the Canon abandon this pattern. But the form of "The Mazarin Stone" or "The Lion's Mane" is not what we expect in a Sherlock Holmes adventure and it should not be what we get in a Sherlock Holmes pastiche.

Pay attention to the minor characters. Mrs. Hudson, for example, is expected. And which of the Scotland Yarders should it be? The time period of the story may help determine that. Early in the Canonical tales, it is most likely to be Gregson or Lestrade or both; later on, the promising young Stanley Hopkins is often on the case.

But it is Holmes who must hold center stage. And he must act Sherlockian. You know his methods, and they do *not* include cocaine. They consist of:

- tobacco, especially on a "three-pipe problem;"
- the lens – a minute examination of scratches, footprints, marks in the dust, etc.;
- violin music, more often than not some composition or improvisation by Sherlock Holmes;
- chemical analysis;
- analytical deduction (actually induction, as he practiced it);
- bouts of contemplation;
- analogy to previous cases (many of them, sadly, unrecorded adventures of Sherlock Holmes), often supported newspaper clippings or by other documentation from the commonplace books with their curious indexing system;
- feverish energy, during which Holmes becomes like a foxhound, "eyes shining and cheeks tinged with colour;"
- special knowledge, often a subject upon which Holmes has written a monograph;
- disguises perfect enough to fool even Dr. Watson – over and over again.

Not all of these methods are used in every story, of course, but often more than one is.

If you know and love Sherlock Holmes enough to indulge in the craft of pastiche writing, you probably already have an instinctive feel for the shape such a story should take. But if you haven't read Ronald A. Knox's seminal "Studies in the Literature of Sherlock Holmes" recently, you may be surprised at how closely he defines the pattern of the typical Sherlock Holmes story.

The classic Knox essay winds up being a virtual eleven-point blueprint for pastiche writing. Only *A Study in Scarlet* has all eleven elements identified by Monsignor Knox, but most stories in the Canon have at least five. Those elements are:

(1) a homely Baker Street scene to start, with invaluable personal touches and sometimes a demonstration by the detective or reference by either Holmes or Watson to an untold tale of Sherlock Holmes;

(2) the client's statement of the case;

(3) energetic personal investigation by Holmes and Watson, often including the famous floor-walk on hands and knees;

(4) refutation by Holmes of the Scotland Yard theory;

(5) a few stray hints to the police, which they never adopt;

(6) Holmes tells the true course of the case to Dr. Watson as he sees it, but is sometimes wrong;

(7) questioning of the victim's relatives, dependents, and others, along with visits to the Records Office, and various investigations in disguise;

(8) the criminal is caught or exposed;

(9) the criminal confesses;

(10) Holmes describes the clues and how he followed them;

(11) the conclusion, often involving a quotation from some standard author.

This is the skeleton of a classic Sherlock Holmes story. You need only a plot to give it flesh and blood.

I prefer stories that don't contradict the known facts of Sherlock Holmes as presented in the Canon. The *Seven-Per-Cent Solution*, to cite one obvious and well-known example, shatters this injunction, as have many other pastiches. I don't like such stories, but perhaps you do. It is a matter of taste.

In that same spirit, I wish to call your attention to a number of other practices that, to my taste, are often disappointing in pastiches:

The appearance or mention of real people or well-known fictional characters of Holmes's day are overdone. Almost every pastiche, in fact, includes them. In the Canon, by contrast, Watson always disguises the victims, villains and minor players of his little dramas, although sometimes thinly.

Mycroft Holmes appears too predictably. Pastiche writers are understandably smitten by this imposing figure. Aren't we all? My objection isn't so much to having him in any one story. It is the cumulative effect of seeing him in nearly every pastiche that bothers me.

References to Holmes as "great" or "famous" are jarring to me. That's a Sherlockian writing, not Watson. The good doctor usually calls Holmes "my friend," "my companion," or simply "Sherlock Holmes."

The recently-discovered-manuscript ploy has grown threadbare with use. By now these hitherto unpublished Watson manuscripts, discovered in attics and bank vaults from London to New England, must number in the hundreds. Even Nigel Bruce's Watson couldn't lose that many manuscripts!

Repeated references to other stories in the Canon strike a false note. Yes, Watson did make such references on occasion, but always briefly – in no more than a few words.

Any title using the name of Sherlock Holmes, the word "case," or even (in a book-length story) the word "adventure" is highly un-Canonical and a turn-off from the start.

Footnotes don't work. They are often added to lend verisimilitude to the conceit that this is a recently discovered manuscript. The idea is that the footnotes are notations from scholars to help a modern audience understand what would have been obvious to earlier generations. Instead, the departure from Canonical form (footnotes are used only in the American section of *A Study Scarlet*) just calls attention to fact that this is a pastiche.

These are just my peeves, of course. I wouldn't do any of these things in a pastiche. But if you want to, go ahead. It's your story. It's not mine – and it's not Dr. Watson's.

THE PECULIAR PERSECUTION OF JOHN VINCENT HARDEN

In 1988, Mysteries from the Yard Bookstore in Yellow Springs, Ohio, held a contest for the best original Sherlockian pastiche. I had never written a pastiche, but the prize of a $100 gift certificate at the bookstore was irresistible to me. I entered and, as noted earlier, won. Like many pastiche writers, I drew my inspiration from one of the many unwritten adventures of Sherlock Holmes referred to in the Canon. And I deliberately chose one of the more obscure such references. (Who needs yet another "Giant Rat of Sumatra"?) In "The Adventure of the Solitary Cyclist," we read of Holmes "immersed in a very abstruse and complicated problem concerning the peculiar persecution to which John Vincent Harden, the well known tobacco millionaire, had been subjected." That meager mention left me a lot of room to maneuver. I started by naming almost every character, except for the Canonical ones, after a member of the Tankerville Club. Some of those names you have encountered already in the introductory essay. Three others have gone beyond the Reichenbach since this tale was written. I offer this story in memory of those late friends – William (Bill) Russell, Norma Holt and Evelyn Weber. The later was in real life a charmingly eccentric elderly woman. The story was first printed, with the permission of the Conan Doyle estate, in The Sherlock Holmes Review *in 1990, Volume 2, Numbers 3 and 4. I also have adapted the story into a radio play, which has been formed by Sherlockian groups as readers' theater.*

In reviewing my notes of the many singular adventures shared with my friend Sherlock Holmes, I have often been struck by the remarkable number that concerned themselves with the doings of Americans.

Many such cases I have already presented to a long-suffering public. The Lauriston Gardens mystery and the tragedy of Birlstone, to name but two, were present-day crimes whose seeds were sown long ago in the fertile soil of the American continent.

Other incidents are doubtless too familiar to my readers to require further chronicling here. No one acquainted with the curious case of the bareback rider or with the horrifying immolation of the straw doll, which defeated the official police of three continents, could soon forget the chilling details.

There remain, however, some few examples of what might be called my friend's "American connexions" which deserve a wider audience. (Let those responsible for the distasteful episode of the cajun cook be forewarned.) Surely any one of these hitherto uncelebrated problems would be of sufficient interest to engage the reader, else they would not have engaged Mr. Sherlock Holmes. None, however, was more fantastic than the peculiar persecution of John Vincent Harden.

It was mid-April of 1895. The fresh breezes of early spring blew through Baker Street, seeming to sweep away the crime and disease of the great city and make everything new again. After a frenzied round of professional calls in the morning and early afternoon, brought on by so sudden a change in the weather, I sat exhausted beside the unlit fireplace nodding over a medical journal. Sherlock Holmes, newly returned to our quarters in the guise of a simple fisherman, was absorbed in a microscopic examination of a peculiar red clay tracked in on his boots. We spoke but seldom, and such were the relations between us in those days that little talk was necessary.

Accustomed as we were to callers at all hours, the intrusion of our landlady into this comfortable scene was not entirely surprising.

"A gentleman to see you," Mrs. Hudson told Holmes.

Sherlock Holmes took the card proffered on a silver tray. He held it up for me to read: "John Vincent Harden, Esq."

"A gentleman, indeed," said Holmes, fingering the nondescript white card as Mrs. Hudson withdrew. "A wealthy American, Watson. Proud, but not haughty, I should judge."

"This is too much, Holmes!" I protested. "Surely even you could scarcely draw such profound inferences from a mere piece of pasteboard."

"Once again you disappoint me, Watson. I assure you my little profile of Mr. John Vincent Harden is written here in black and white, if only you know how to read it: The paper. The engraving. The ink. The whole tone of this tiny document – powerful, but understated. It is much in the American style. And here is our visitor to prove out our modest inferences."

Holmes unfolded his long, lean body and rose to meet the prospective client's outstretched hand. John Vincent Harden was a short but powerfully built man wearing an expensive white linen suit, torn and stained from some recent altercation, and carrying a walking stick. He affected a large, graying mustache in the fashion of the American General Burnside. I put his age in the middle 50s, but when he gripped my hand it was with the strength of one decades younger.

"Mr. Holmes, I'll come straight to the point," said he, in the forthright manner of one who could do naught else. "I hear tell you're the best."

"Indeed? Friend Watson here has spread the news of my poor powers farther than I had suspected if I am so famous in – Tennessee, perhaps?"

"Kentucky, sir."

"Indeed? I should have thought a trifle farther south. That explains, then, why you fought on the victorious Northern side in the American Civil War. Perhaps the late unpleasantness had something to do with your uncertain fortunes, for it is obvious that you were born into great wealth, lost it, but regained substantial means through your own labours."

John Vincent Harden tightened his grip on the walking stick. "You're good, all right. Damned good. Unless somebody told you about me."

"I assure you I never heard your name until your card announced you five minutes ago, Mr. Harden. That card and you yourself told me all that I know of you. The 'GAR' emblem on the watch fob in your waistcoat pocket stands for 'Grand Army of the Republic,' does it not? Your military bearing would have ended any doubt I may have entertained. The gold watch which you consulted upon entering this room is old, but clearly valuable. An heirloom, then, of a wealthy family. Yet your hands are scarred, calloused. You have done manual labor, though not recently. And those efforts have paid off handsomely, for your dress – though tattered by whatever misadventure has brought you into these chambers – tells me you are wealthy once more."

"I'm rich enough, all right, but let's get down to cases. I'm here because I'm damned scared."

The frank admission of fright, coming from this man of such obvious moral and physical strength, sent a chill through the warm sitting room. I believe that even Sherlock Holmes, the least fanciful of men, must have felt it. He leaned forward.

"Pray tell your story from the beginning, leaving out nothing. As you have seen, I am one who can make much of little things."

"Well, sir, as for my early life, you seem to know a good deal already. I grew up on my family's tobacco plantation, Whitecrest, thirty miles southwest of Lexington. We owned a hundred and twenty-five slaves. When the War Between the States broke out back in '61, the Commonwealth of Kentucky was badly split. Both Jeff Davis and Abe Lincoln were born in our state, you understand. Officially, Kentucky stayed with Lincoln and the Union, and that's where I saw my duty. I joined the army, fought at Gettysburg, rose to the rank of Colonel. But back at home, a lot of friends – even family – were joining the Rebs. Whitecrest was fair game for Rebel looters and marauders. When I returned from the war, there wasn't much left of it. The house was a shambles. The slaves were gone. My mother was dead. My father didn't recognize me. My brother – he was younger than I – had run off to join Morgan's Raiders and never made it back.

"Mr. Holmes, that was thirty years ago, but not a day has gone by since that I haven't remembered the vow I made to myself then: The Rebs couldn't beat Grant and they weren't going to beat me. I would start over. I would plant tobacco with my own two hands if I had to. And I would make my own fortune. There were hard years, sir. Many of them. The harder they got, the harder I got. Yes, I am a hard man, but a fair man. And a successful one, for I fulfilled that vow."

Holmes stirred from his lounging position and lit his clay pipe. "And yet your life has not been without sadness."

The tobacco millionaire stared at the floor, his clear blue eyes seeing far away as he replied in a dull voice: "I married a wonderful woman, sir. Norma brought grace and culture to Whitecrest. Even taught a hard man like me to appreciate your Mr. Shakespeare. She was carried away by consumption in '81. Ophelia, our daughter, is the joy of my life – the reason I want to keep living."

For all the forced gruffness with which he said these last words, our visitor's voice was at the point of breaking and there was a wildness in his eyes. I handed him a glass of brandy and a cigar, medicines for melancholy, as Holmes pressed on. "It is only in England that you have become preoccupied with such thoughts, I perceive."

"That's true enough, sir," John Vincent Harden conceded, setting down his walking stick to take a firm grip on the cigar in one hand and the brandy in the other. "All has gone well for me in my own element these recent years. I have reared Ophelia to a fine young woman of eighteen. She is to be married this fall to a young man of great promise. Her mother would be proud."

"You approve of the match, then?"

"In every degree, sir. Stephen – Mr. Stephen Winter – comes from a fine old Lexington family. And yet I felt that before she entered the married state Ophelia ought to see the world in an extended stay abroad. We arrived in London nine weeks ago. For the first two months, we enjoyed the sites of your great city immensely. Then, six days go, I became the object of what I can only regard as a persecution, fanciful though the notion may seem. Ophelia and I returned to our hotel, the Langham, that afternoon after seeing Mr. Irving in *Hamlet* – my Norma's favorite play – at the Adelphi Theatre."

"Something was missing?" I conjectured.

John Vincent Harden almost chuckled. "I suppose you could say our room was missing, in a manner of speaking. It had been rented out to someone else! The room clerk, a man named Weber whom I'd never seen before, solemnly assured me that not three hours previously I had paid our bill and departed with my luggage and my daughter. Ophelia and I had to spend two days in a little cubbyhole before a proper room was available to us. Meanwhile, we had to replace all the clothing in our luggage. Damned nuisance. I almost quit England right then, but Ophelia wouldn't have it.

"The clerk and the hotel manager acted as if I were a madman. I might have thought them right if Ophelia hadn't assured me I had indeed been with her the entire day. Someone else checked us out of that hotel, Mr. Holmes. Someone who looked and sounded just like me."

The American sat back and drank deeply from his brandy.

Holmes smoked in silence.

"But this is fantastic!" I cried. "It recalls nothing so much as Poe's unearthly story of the two William Wilsons."

"Tut-tut, Watson. Let us not be fanciful. Surely there are parallels enough in the commonplace books" – Holmes indicated their place on our shelves – "without turning to the supernatural for a solution to this mystery. The affair of the missing tobacco shop at Vienna in '87 suggests itself immediately. There was also that dangerous little business at Montpellier two years ago in which I was of some assistance to M. Luttmer of the Sureté. And certainly you, Watson, remember the rather comic incident of diminutive love rivals of the Brandenburg Circus."

"Certainly. But I fail to see – "

"Precisely," said Holmes. "You fail to see."

"There's more," our visitor interrupted, speaking in the dull tones of a man almost defeated. "Three days ago I received at the Langham this wire from my man Lear, who is operating Whitecrest in my absence."

He handed the wire to my companion, who quickly scanned its few words, then handed it on to me. It read:

BIG PROBLEM WITH SPRING PLANTING. URGENT YOU RETURN IMMEDIATELY. LEAR

"Well, sir, you may be assured I am not in the habit of taking instructions from my employees without so much as asking a few questions first," the Kentuckian resumed. "I wired right back inquiring the exact nature of this 'problem.' Went straight to the Wigmore Street telegraph office to send it myself. Late that evening I received this reply."

The second wire was even more succinct:

WHAT PROBLEM? E. LEAR

"Lear never sent that first wire, Mr. Holmes," said John Vincent Harden. "It was a hoax."

"Surely this is only some ill-conceived joke," I observed.

"I might have thought so myself, Doctor, but for what occurred within this very hour to leave my clothing in the sorry state you see before you. I was just leaving the Langham to spend the late afternoon hours at the galleries. Scarcely had I stepped off the curb before I heard a terrible clatter. It was a four-wheeled cab bearing down on me with the speed of a runaway. But it was no runaway, gentlemen. The driver was urging the horses forward, not trying to reign them in. The man was bent on running me down. I was frozen with terror. When I finally did move, I tripped. It seemed I lay in that street for hours waiting to be crushed beneath the onrush of horses' hooves. Only the quick action of a brave young Englishman saved me."

John Vincent Harden pulled a large bandana from his back pocket and mopped his perspiring brow.

"And your daughter?" asked Sherlock Holmes.

"Ophelia is resting in her room. She knows nothing of this murderous incident – nor will she."

"I see." Holmes leaned back, pressing his lean fingertips together. "And the man driving the cab, what did he look like?"

The millionaire shook his head. "I was looking at those horses, sir, not at the driver." His voice sunk to a near-whisper. "I was looking at death."

"Whom do you suspect, then?"

"No one, for I know no one in England. Well, only that wild-eyed poet friend of my daughter, Paul Herbert. Rash young fellow. Runs with that Oscar Wilde crowd. Just this afternoon I told him flat-out I didn't want Ophelia mixing with the likes of him. Stood his ground like a man, I'll give him that. Thought he was going to hit me right there in the lobby of the Langham. Say, do you suppose – "

"I suppose nothing," said Sherlock Holmes. "I deduce."

"You have a clew, then?"

"I am very close to having a solution."

"What!" Our visitor fairly bolted out of his seat. "Without moving from your chair? Pardon my skepticism, sir, but that's – that's incredible!"

"It is commonplace. I noted a few moments ago one or two cases with which I am familiar that seem to point in the direction of a solution. The rest of your narrative only strengthened the parallels. I shall be making inquiries in the next few days to confirm my deductions, but I have every confidence that matters shall be thoroughly resolved by week's end."

"But what shall I do in the meanwhile?"

"Do nothing, Mr. Harden. I shall do the doing. The forces working against you are real, but it isn't your life they want. You are in no real danger."

Two mornings later, rushing towards the High Street in Marylebone on a pre-dawn summons from Stanley

Hopkins of Scotland Yard, I finally induced Sherlock Holmes to explain at least some of his reasoning.

"It was obvious from the first," he said, "that someone wanted our client to return to Kentucky – or at least to leave England. The incident of the hotel room was designed to so disgust him that he would quit the country in a huff, which he very nearly did. The bogus telegram was to lure him away, the apparent attempt on his life to frighten him away. Each time, you see, a somewhat different approach toward the same end. There's the touch of genius in that, Watson. We're up against a worthy opponent this time. Hardly a killer, however."

"But surely, Holmes, you owe it to Mr. Harden to pursue – "

"And pursue I did, Watson. I talked with Evelyn Weber, the clerk at the Langham, this afternoon. Didn't I mention that?" Really, at times Holmes was exasperating. "This Weber is a stooped fellow with a thick mustache. Squints at you through his spectacles. 'Mr. Harden checked out right enough,' says he, 'no matter how he tells the tale.' I have also wired the Lexington, Kentucky, police with two vital questions. Ah, here we are. Let's see what compels friend Hopkins to roust us out of our beds at this hour of the morning."

Stanley Hopkins was in those days a promising young official detective in whose career Sherlock Holmes had taken a great interest. One of his greatest assets, I had always suspected, was that he knew when to call on Holmes for help.

"It's a rum business, Mr. Holmes," said he, leading us into the main room of William Russell's cluttered bookshop. The body of a small man lay outstretched there on the floor, within feet of a wall of bookshelves. Beneath his extended hand, as if he had just pulled it off a shelf, lay an ancient bound edition of *Hamlet.* From his back protruded a silver-handled knife.

"Mr. Russell here" – Hopkins nodded toward an old man with long white hair and a beard like Father Christmas – "lives upstairs. He found this corpse lying here just like this when he came down this morning. I warned everybody not to touch anything until you arrived, sir. The peculiar thing is, Mr. Russell says he's never seen the man before. We are inclined to believe Mr. Russell, he being a well-known and well respected businessman in this neighborhood. So what the devil is this mysterious Mr. Unknown Bloke doing getting himself murdered on Mr. Russell's floor during the night?"

He seemed to take this unfortunate occurrence as almost a personal affront.

Eager as a bloodhound, Holmes dropped to the floor and began examining the dusty area around the body with his lens. His eyes shone and his pale cheeks gained colour. He was in his element: "A falling-out among thieves suggests itself immediately, of course. Two thieves came in; only one left. But this man's dress – "

Holmes uttered a strangled cry as his examination of the body brought him face to face with the dead man. "I am an old woman, Watson! I am Lestrade's idiot nephew! I am not competent to farm bees on the Sussex Downs! Hopkins, we know this man. His name is John Vincent Harden."

Seldom have I seen my notoriously moody friend as melancholy as in the following twelve hours. He smoked prodigiously, scraped out mournful sounds on his violin, and scarcely acknowledged my existence.

"If you won't tell me your conclusions about this case," I said bitterly, "at least tell Stanley Hopkins."

"Soon enough," he replied tersely. "A few more days can't hurt now."

In this, however, Holmes was in error, as became apparent that evening with the arrival in our quarters of Miss Ophelia Harden.

"The police have made an awful mistake, Mr. Holmes," she said. "They have arrested Paul – my friend, Mr. Herbert."

Miss Harden was a handsome, full-figured young lady fashionably dressed in pale colours to accent her blonde hair and blue eyes. Though small, such was the force of her character that few would have labeled her "dainty."

"This is grief piled upon grief, as if Father's death were not horror enough," she wailed. "You must do something!"

Holmes regarded her through half-lidded eyes. "Tell me, Miss Harden, by what idiotic logic did the police decide to arrest young Herbert?"

"He and Father had strong words in public." She lowered her eyes. "They were arguing about me, of course."

"Of course. Your father mentioned the altercation during our meeting. He also made it quite clear that he did not approve of your poetic friend."

"Father thought Mr. Herbert too young, too brash, too immature and thoroughly lacking in prospects. And he was right on every point! Oh, Mr. Holmes, Paul needs the steadying hand of someone like me, even though I am two years the younger."

"And your fiancé?"

"Mr. Winter is perfect in every way, I suppose. He is handsome, tall, wealthy, charming – and, of course, boringly respectable. He may desire my affection and my company, but he doesn't need them the way Paul does. I am fond of him, but not nearly so fond as Father is – was. I was quite undisturbed at writing him about my developing feelings for Paul."

Holmes threw up his arms. "Surely even the Scotland Yarders don't find a murder case against your Mr. Herbert in all of this?"

"Well, there is one other thing against Paul, Mr. Holmes. It's that bookshop where they found Father's body. Paul works there."

Through the kind offices of Stanley Hopkins, we were permitted to interview Paul Herbert in his cell at the Bow Street police station the next morning.

"As God is my witness, Mr. Holmes – if there is a God, which I doubt – I wouldn't have blunted my knife on that benighted man," he proclaimed.

He was a flush-faced, red-haired youth about my own height, pacing the small cell with a nervous energy akin to that of Holmes in one of his bloodhound humours.

"It was your knife, then?" Holmes asked, seeming surprised.

"I don't even own a knife," the young poet snapped. "That was just a figure of speech."

"We have yet to determine the ownership of the knife," Stanley Hopkins told Holmes, somewhat stiffly. "But how much proof do we need? The victim was found dead in the accused's place of employment just a few days after a frightful row between the two of them in the lobby of the Langham Hotel, observed by the hotel staff. He might as well have carved his initials in the man."

Paul Herbert sniffed. "Being arrested for murder at least has a certain dignity. Now you're saying I'm bloody stupid. That's bloody insulting!"

"Watch your tongue, young man," Hopkins chided. "Of course he didn't plan to leave the body there, Mr. Holmes. The way we at the Yard have it figured, the accused here lured Mr. Harden to the bookshop in the late evening to kill him. Miss Harden confirms her father received some sort of message at the hotel that night. He rushed out, refusing to tell her where he was going. He never came back. Mr. Herbert killed him as planned. Things only began to go wrong when something stopped him from moving the body. It was probably the shop owner, Mr. Russell, coming down the stairs."

"But Harden left his hotel in the evening and was killed then," Holmes objected. "Russell didn't find the body until this morning."

"Merely a detail, Mr. Holmes."

"Details are everything, Hopkins. How many times must I tell you that? Now, how did Herbert here get into the bookshop after hours?"

"When he isn't writing poems, he sells books. As a long-time, trusted employee of William Russell – almost like a son, we understand – he has a key to the shop. Russell told us that. Didn't want to, but we got it out of him."

"*Had* a key," Paul Herbert spat, his face more flushed than ever. "I told you I was set upon by a ruffian last night and knocked out. When I woke up, nothing seemed to be missing. I was puzzled as the devil. Then I was brought here on this absurd charge and the official hooligans searched me for the key to the shop. That's when I discovered it was gone."

"Very convenient," Hopkins said heavily. "We'll find it yet."

"Doubtless," said Holmes. "One further point, however: Have you arrived at a theory explaining why John Vincent Harden used his last ounce of strength to grasp a copy of *Hamlet*, a play he had seen a few afternoons previously? One might have thought he was attempting to indicate his killer, and yet there is no murdering poet in the work as I recall it."

"There is, however, a young lady named Ophelia," Hopkins rejoined smartly. "We reckon Mr. Harden's last thoughts were of the poor deluded daughter he tried to protect from this swine. Really, Mr. Holmes, we of the official force seem to have done rather well without you this time. Is there any little point we may have missed?"

Holmes stroked his chin. "Let us see, Hopkins. You have missed the real killer, the real motive, and, oh yes, the real country."

Stanley Hopkins stood open-mouthed. "Country, sir? I'm afraid I don't – "

"No, you don't. The origin and the solution of this crime lie in America, Hopkins. If you fail to grasp that, you are hopeless."

The truth of these words was quickly borne out. Waiting for us back at 221B when we returned from the police station was a telegram. "This tears it, Watson!" Holmes exclaimed, tossing me the wire. "We have our man."

The wire read:

LEAR ON JOB. WINTER UNSEEN ONE WEEK. R.J. SENTER, POLICE CHIEF, LEXINGTON, KY., USA

"Our bird will fly as soon as possible now that Herbert is headed for the dock. He needed to stay in London only long enough to make suitably incriminating testimony against our young poet. Grab your service revolver, Watson, for we haven't a moment to lose." Holmes was already on his way back out the door. "I'll tell Billy to have Hopkins meet us there with a pair of strong bracelets."

"By all that is holy, meet us where?" I shouted after him.

"At the Langham, of course."

"This is beyond me, Holmes!" I cried.

"No doubt."

The Langham remains one of the grandest of London's grand hotels. Holmes marched up to the magnificent front desk and hailed the clerk, a stooped figure of uncertain age hidden behind a thick, sandy mustache. The clerk peered at us through round spectacles, squinting. "Oh, hello, Mr. – Holmes, was it?"

He spoke in an indefinable Colonial accent, which I make no attempt to reproduce – some strange cross-breeding of South African and Australian, it seemed to me.

"Frightful goings-on since our little chat," he said. "Mr. Harden showing up dead and all, naught but a couple days after that awful row with Mr. Herbert right here in the lobby." He lowered his voice to a conspiratorial whisper. "They were both mad as hatters, if you ask me."

Holmes leaned forward. "Well, Weber, I'm quite sure you told the gentlemen from the Yard – Oh, excuse me." In an uncharacteristically clumsy move, Holmes had managed to knock the clerk's spectacles clean off his face.

"Terribly sorry," Holmes said, holding the lenses out at eye level. "But do you know, I've found that clear glass like this can scarcely hope to improve the vision anyway."

Like a frightened rabbit, Weber looked nervously from one to the other of us, then bolted. Holmes dived after, with me close behind. The crowd in the great lobby was sparse, giving the villain a nearly open field – but us one as well. Across the huge expanse we pursued him, only occasionally jostling a guest or two. We narrowed the gap but couldn't quite close it. Our prey was within an arm's length of a side entrance when the door unexpectedly swung open. Weber had up such a head of steam there was little he could do save collide with the newcomer.

"Here now – what's the hurry?" that person asked, grabbing Weber by the scruff of the neck.

"Hold him, Hopkins!" Holmes cried, for it was indeed our young friend from Scotland Yard who stood holding the clerk.

Hopkins quickly clamped a set of handcuffs on his captive even as I leveled my revolver for good measure.

"Who is this man, Mr. Holmes?" Hopkins demanded.

"The persecutor and killer of John Vincent Harden – Mr. Stephen Winter."

So identified, the man gave up all pretensions of being that which he was not. He shed the unnatural stoop of the hotel clerk, showing his true rather considerable height. He ripped off his mustache, revealing it to be as false as his spectacles. As he addressed us in his own Southern American voice, I realized that the unusual accent of the clerk Weber was but an unsuccessful attempt to sound English.

"All right, fellows," said he, in the coolest possible tones. "I fought the good fight but I know when I'm licked. I'm guilty as sin and you've won the right to hang me fair and square. And come to that, I think maybe I'd rather be dead in England than poor in Kentucky anyway." He straightened his tie. "Though as for blame, gentlemen, it's really Colonel Harden's fault as much as mine, don't you see? I never in the world had it in mind to kill him, but he forced me to. When I checked him and Ophelia out of the hotel, he didn't leave England. When I handed him that phony wire telling him to return to Whitecrest, he couldn't just take it at face value and go. And when I tried to scare him away by half running over him with a rented four-wheeler, he went to see you instead, Mr. Holmes. The man was just too stubborn to live."

"I had a fair idea of the game you were playing early on," said Holmes, "but I never thought you'd turn over the death card."

"That's because you didn't know how desperate I am. No one did."

"But why did you want Harden out of England so badly?" Hopkins asked.

"Not Harden," Holmes responded. "Miss Harden, Winter's fiancé."

"She wouldn't have been my fiancé much longer if she'd stayed in England," Winter said. "I could tell that from the way she wrote about this Herbert fellow in her letters. But I could also that tell her father opposed any possible match between the two. He wanted her to marry well. I felt certain that if I could pull them apart for a few months, the Colonel would prevail and Ophelia and I would be safely wed."

"So it was an affair of the heart," the police detective said.

Holmes tutted. "Still the romantic, Hopkins? Ah, well, you are young. An affair of the pocketbook, more likely."

Stephen Winter nodded affably. "Alas, gentlemen, I wish I could claim a more noble motivation, but once again you have me. The family fortune I inherited was a respectable one, but I am afraid that my penchant for Kentucky horses has taken a devastating toll on my financial position. Even my home is heavily mortgaged, though no one knew it. Marriage to a wealthy woman seemed the only practical solution. Having conducted my affairs discreetly so as to avoid public scandal and maintain my reputation, I was considered a good catch. Ophelia was available and initially willing. Her father, as you know, approved. Then they came to England and disaster loomed. I spent most of my dwindling resources following them here to preserve my marriage hopes. It was one gamble I had to win, for I had risked all. Once here, I became Evelyn Weber, hotel clerk. In that guise, working at this hotel, I could keep track of the

Hardens and be in a good position to carry out my schemes for encouraging their departure from England. I had little fear of being recognized by them, for people our sort don't really notice people of the sort I was made out to be.

"If only Colonel Harden hadn't been so stubborn it would have worked. Well, what can you expect of a Union man? I reluctantly concluded that nothing short of her father's death would send Ophelia scurrying back to Whitecrest. Fortunately, Providence blessed me with a public argument between the Colonel and my rival, Paul Herbert. As Evelyn Weber, I would call police attention to the damning event before I mysteriously disappeared. Others saw it happen, too, so even Ophelia couldn't deny it. If Colonel Harden were murdered, surely that young hothead would be the chief suspect. And if he were hanged, then all my troubles would be over for sure. I would be the reliable suitor rushing to comfort Ophelia in her hour of need, making us all the closer.

"But I had to be sure the case against Herbert was a tight one. So I followed him, learned as much as I could about him. When I saw him using a key of his own to close up the bookshop, I conceived a brilliant idea: Lure the Colonel into the shop with a note promising some dirt about young Herbert, distract his attention, stick a knife in his back and leave the body to be found in the morning. Who would believe Herbert's cock and bull story of the key being stolen? Certainly not Scotland Yard. Of course, I took back from his body the note that brought Colonel Harden to the bookshop.

"You know, gentlemen, I rather liked Ophelia's father after a fashion, despite his stubbornness and his Union sympathies. After all, he was on my side. I did so hate to kill him. Rather liked Ophelia, too, come to that."

The killer smiled.

"The key facts were in our hands from the very first," Sherlock Holmes explained at Baker Street the following evening after a hearty meal at Simpson's. "I was convinced that the killer was whoever lay behind the peculiar persecution of John Vincent Harden. Two antagonists would be too much of a coincidence. Colonel Harden believed he knew no one in England except Paul Herbert, who had no conceivable reason for wanting the Hardens to leave the country – quite the contrary, in fact. The answer, then, as I suggested to Hopkins, lay in America. Who there might benefit from driving the Hardens out of the country? The presence of an English love rival to Miss Harden's fiancé made Stephen Winter a suspect immediately. No such motivation was readily apparent for Lear, the major domo of Whitecrest Plantation, but he could not be ruled out since his name was connected with what turned out to be a seemingly spurious wire from America.

"One of these men, it seemed likely, was John Vincent Harden's mysterious persecutor – either in person or through an agent in England. I sent a wire of my own to Kentucky to determine whether either was off the scene. By the time I received a reply that confirmed my earliest suspicions of Miss Harden's beau, I was already fairly certain of the guise under which he was operating in this country.

"The first of the incidents plaguing Harden – the story of the apparent *Doppelganger* who checked the Hardens out of their rooms at the Langham – was mysterious only if the room clerk, a man Harden had never seen before, had told the truth. Assume that he lied and the mystery evaporated. It all hinged, then, on Evelyn Weber. Now consider the bogus telegram from Lear. It was presented to Harden at the hotel – presumably by a bellboy who could well have received it from the room clerk. Harden sent his follow-up wire from the Wigmore Street telegraph office, where Weber never knew of it. The response came back the following evening, when Weber was off duty. That's the only reason Harden ever saw it. The murderous attack of the four-wheeler, I need hardy add, occurred just outside the hotel. Everything came back to the Langham and, by inference, to Weber. Clearly, he was also one of the hotel staff who overheard the heated dispute in the lobby between Messers Harden and Herbert – putting him in an excellent position to blame the former's death on the latter. Weber could have been merely an agent for Winter, of course, but the plain glass spectacles were a transparent disguise."

Holmes sat back in his chair.

"And so ends another successful case for my annals," I commented.

"The case was indeed a great success," Holmes said bitterly. "Only the client died. No, Watson, I have scarcely covered myself with glory in this one. If you should ever chance to chronicle this adventure, let it be as the folly of an over-celebrated sleuthhound, not as some sort of triumph."

He picked up his violin and commenced to scratch out a melancholy series of notes that seemed to match his mood.

"Holmes!" I cried after enduring some minutes of this. "The *Hamlet*! What in the world was the significance of the book John Vincent Harden grabbed in his final moment? You asked Hopkins for his theory, but you never gave your own."

"Didn't I? Well, we can never know the truth for sure," said Sherlock Holmes, looking up from his instrument. "But having met the charming Stephen Winter, perhaps the answer lies in Act I, Scene V, if I recall correctly – 'meet it is I set it down/That one may smile, and smile, and be a villain.' "

THE ADVENTURE OF THE AMATEUR PLAYERS

My first attempts to write novel-length detective fiction in the early 1980s was a series for kids about a group of young sleuths who called themselves the Deerstalker Club. The creator and leader of the club, Toby Motherwell, bore more than a passing resemblance to a boyhood friend, the late Ralph Eppensteiner, in his precocious vocabulary and rather formal speech pattern. The narrator, Billy Piccolo, was the son of a newspaper journalist, which happened to be my profession at the time. Ralph "Ski" Wysnewski was a budding actor. Perhaps my favorite character was Sara Moon, who is every bit as smart as Toby and has a knack for pricking his pomposity with a few well-chosen words of her own. These characters are not fully fleshed out in the limited space of the story that follows, but it is a Sherlockian mystery. The story was inspired by a cartoon, which I cannot describe without giving away the ending. I wrote it at the same time as the novels. Like them, it was never published.

The night of the cast party was cold and wet. That was okay while we were snug in the theater watching the play *Sherlock Holmes.* The pounding rhythm of the rain even added to the atmosphere of the play. But it sure made the two hundred yard dash from the Grubb Street Theater to Roger Pressler's house miserable. Icy rain beat at our legs beneath our upraised umbrellas.

"Wretched!" Toby Motherwell called it as we sloshed through soggy grass.

"I bet it'll be cozy at Mr. Pressler's party, though," Sara Moon said.

Our tall friend Ralph Wysnewski – "Ski" to us – was back at the theater getting out of his makeup. He played Sherlock Holmes's page, Billy.

I'm a Billy, too – Billy Piccolo.

We were among the first to get to Mr. Pressler's house, but before long everyone from the play seemed to be there. They left their umbrellas on the porch and crowded around the roaring fire in the Pressler living room.

Roger Pressler himself, founder of the amateur theater group and star of *Sherlock Holmes*, was the center of attention. He still wore Toby's deerstalker hat, lent to him for the run of the play. His long legs were damp, but not his spirits.

"What an audience!" he crowed. "We'll make enough money on this production to save the Grubb Street Players!"

He turned to Toby, Sara, Ski and me. "We owe a lot to you, Toby. I'm sure all the attention from the Deerstalker Club connection sold tickets."

"A few perhaps," Toby mumbled.

I looked away. Watching Toby Motherwell being modest was just too painful.

Anyway, Mr. Pressler was right. The Deerstalker Club – that's the four of us – had picked up a lot of publicity solving mysteries the previous summer. And when Ski landed a part in *Sherlock Holmes* and Toby lent his Holmes expertise (and deerstalker) to the production, the publicity rubbed off on the Grubb Street Players.

But Sara frowned. "If this play is that important to you, your treasury must really be running low."

Roger Pressler nodded. "If we hadn't done well with this play, we would have had to give up our lease on the theater."

"You don't own it?" Toby asked.

"Right. That's our landlord over there."

Mr. Pressler pointed across the room to a stout, bearded man carrying a folded-up umbrella as though it were a walking stick. He was drenched all over, with sopping wet hair hanging in his eyes.

"His name is Moses Gamble," Mr. Pressler said. "His great-grandfather, Solomon Gamble, was a railroad millionaire who built the theater for amateur magic shows. The place sat unused for years after the family fell on harder times. I leased it from Moses' father, the late Jonah Gamble, when we started the Grub Street Players five years ago."

"If we don't make the lease payments," Ski said, "Moses can take it over."

"But what would he do with it?" I asked.

"Probably turn it into condominiums," Mr. Pressler said. "That's what he did with the rest of old Solomon's property. I guess he's on his way to building the second great Gamble fortune."

"Roger!" A chunky, grey-haired woman shouted his name. It was Mary Knight, the ticket seller, rushing into the living room. "We've been robbed!"

Everybody tried to talk at once. Roger Pressler finally got them quieted down so Mrs. Knight could tell her story:

"The cash box with the ticket money was locked in the supply room during the play, like always. After the play, I did a few chores, then picked up the cash box so I could count the money later. But it felt too light. It was empty!"

Roger Pressler moaned. "Ruined! We're ruined for sure now!"

"Net yet," Toby Motherwell counted. "Not with the Deerstalker Club on the case." His round face came alive. "Was the cash box locked?"

Mrs. Knight nodded. "But the lock was broken."

"How about the supply room?"

"Well it – Yes! I had to use my key to open it."

"Who else had a key?"

"I did." That was Fred Leggin, the Professor Moriarty of the play. "I'm the treasurer of the Players."

"And I'm in charge of supplies, so I have a key, too," said Jenny LeBlond, who really is blond.

"So do I, of course," said Roger Presser.

"Too many keys," Toby snapped. "Any of them could have been copied."

Moses Gamble thumped the floor with his umbrella. "I strongly suggest a search of everyone in this room."

Toby looked around, peering through his round glasses. "No need for a search. I know who took the money and why."

In one swift motion, he grabbed Moses Gamble's umbrella and pushed the button near the handle. The umbrella sprang open. Tiny drops of rain went flying.

And from inside the umbrella it rained, too – hundreds of dollars of U.S. currency.

"It was our simplest case," Toby told Mr. Pressler after everyone else had left.

"Moses Gamble was soaking wet from his head on down – not just on his legs, like us. He carried an umbrella, yet obviously hadn't used it on the long trek here from the theater. There had to be a reason."

"Why would a man as rich as he is stoop to stealing a few hundred dollars?" Ski asked.

"To keep the Grubb Street Players from making their lease payments," Sara Moon said. "That way he could take control of the property and develop it. Condominiums, remember?"

"But the key – " Roger Pressler began.

"Of course Moses Gamble had one," Toby said. "He owns the building."

Roger Pressler took off Toby's deerstalker hat. "Anybody can wear one of these, Toby. But only a few deserve to."

And he held it out to its rightful owner.

THE WRONG CAB

I have always been fascinated by the imaginative power of radio drama. When I was a young boy in the early 1960s, I tuned in weekly to the adventures of insurance investigator Johnny Dollar, perhaps the last of the radio detectives. Now fast forward more than 25 years: In 1988-89 I wrote three radio plays for a project called Dimension Radio Theater, produced in Cincinnati but later carried on National Public Radio. Not surprisingly, perhaps, my first effort involved Sherlock Holmes. It started with a "what if" – "What if I could take over Dr. Watson's role at the side of Sherlock Holmes?" From that sprang a fantasy about a cynical private eye to whom that mysteriously happens. With malice aforethought I named him Dutch Reid. The Reid came from the last name of both the Green Hornet and his great-uncle, the Lone Ranger – two of the greatest heroes of radio's Golden Age. The nickname Dutch came from a former sportscaster named Dutch Reagan, who went on to host "Death Valley Days" and dabble a bit in politics. The Anglo-Indian Club in this play will recall the Tankerville Club, but none of its members are based on real people. Madame Tussaud's is described just as it was in that era. "The Wrong Cab" was first broadcast on Nov. 15, 1988. In the rebroadcast of the entire Dimension Radio Theater series by NPR in 1990, the mellifluous voice of the host for all of the plays belonged to Nick Clooney, father of George.

FORMAT: THEME MUSIC BEGINS AND ENDS

HOST: (Underscore Theme Music): Welcome to Dimension Radio Theater's Production of "The Wrong Cab," written by Daniel M. Andriacco and directed by D. Lynn Myers. Sherlock Holmes was created by Sir Arthur Conan Doyle and appears in stories and novels by him. Grateful acknowledgement is made to Dame Jean Conan Doyle for permission to use the Sherlock Holmes characters in this production.

FADE TO BLACK

SFX: TAXI DOOR CLOSING

AMBI: TAXI CAB – INTERIOR

CAB DRIVER: Where to, gentlemen?

LAFCADIO: 41 Half Moon Street. On a night like this, it ought to be Baker Street.

SFX: ENGINE ROARS TO LIFE/ CAR PULLS AWAY / TRAFFIC NOISES

DUTCH:	With the windows down it's even foggy in here. You still with me, Figg?
LAFCADIO: (Chuckling)	Where would I go? But there's no fog in here.
DUTCH:	Can't see you. Getting a little drowsy.
LAFCADIO:	I shouldn't have bought you those last two drinks, Dutch . . . Dutch . . . Dutch!!! (Voice fades out.)
HOST:	(Underscore theme music) ILLUSION . . . REALITY . . . TWO VERY DIFFERENT THINGS . . . TWO SEPARATE WORLDS, IN FACT. BUT THERE IS A BRIDGE BETWEEN THEM, AND DUTCH REID CROSSED THAT BRIDGE THE NIGHT HE STEPPED INTO THE WRONG CAB. HIS REMARKABLE JOURNEY REALLY BEGAN EARLIER THAT EVENING, AT A MEETING OF A SOCIETY DEDICATED TO THE MEMORY OF SHERLOCK HOLMES.
AMBI:	RESTAURANT / PARTY ROOM – INTERIOR

FOLEY: PARTY NOISES / GLASSES TINKLING / MUTED CONVERSATION / LAUGHTER

MOLLY: You're new, aren't you?

DUTCH: Yeah. I don't even know much about this outfit. Why the name, for instance – the Anglo-Indian Club?

MOLLY: We had to call ourselves something, and the best names were already taken by other Holmes societies.

DUTCH: I've only read a few of those Sherlock Holmes stories. No offense, but I didn't think much of them.

NOAH: Then what brings you here?

DUTCH: Lafcadio Figg. He invited me. Why the hell I agreed to come, I'm still not sure.

SFX: FOOTSTEPS CROSS THE ROOM AND STOP.

LAFCADIO: It could be my charm and persuasive personality, dear boy. However, I think it far more likely that my promise to buy the drinks carried the day. Cheers.

SFX: GLASSES TINKLING.

LAFCADIO: My fellow Sherlockians, may I present Mr. Dutch Reid. One of less distinguished former students from my days at the high school, but the only one to my knowledge who ever became a private detective.

NOAH: I'm impressed. But Holmes was the greatest detective of all. Why don't you share our enthusiasm for him, Mr. Reid?

DUTCH: He just isn't real. I read that story you're going to talk about after dinner, *The Sign of Four*. Here we have a lost treasure, death by poison dart, a pygmy killer and a mad boat chase down the river – all in one case! Give me a break!

BARRY: Hold on a minute, Mr. Reid. Aren't you the guy who was involved in that shootout with Santa Claus at Garloh's Department Store last Christmas? In the ladies underwear department?

DUTCH: Yeah, that was me, kid. Shot him between the bras and the panties. But let me tell you about the case I'm working now. Harry Devereaux and his house both went up in a ball of flames. It's arson. The insurance company suspects the wife. I've been

	sticking to her like flypaper for eight months with nothing to show for it. That's what most real-life detective work is like. Not very romantic.
HARRIET:	But Mr. Reid, we aren't interested in reality. We're interested in atmosphere, character, puzzles.
LAFCADIO:	And puzzles within puzzles.
DUTCH:	What's that supposed to mean?
LAFCADIO:	You'll see.
FORMAT:	THEME MUSIC BEGINS AND ENDS
X-FADE TO:	
AMBI:	PARTY ROOM, LATER
FOLEY:	INDISTINGUISHABLE BACKGROUND CONVERSATION
NARRATOR (DUTCH):	THE ROAST BEEF WAS PASSABLE. IT WAS ALL THAT SHERLOCK HOLMES TALK AFTER DINNER THAT I FOUND HARD TO SWALLOW.
NOAH:	One thing we haven't mentioned yet is the famous enigma of Dr.

	Watson's wound. In *A Study in Scarlet*, Watson writes about being wounded in the arm. But here in *The Sign of Four*, seven years later, the wound is in his leg. How do we explain that?
BARRY:	Obviously Watson was bent over when he was wounded. The same bullet passed through both his leg and his arm!
FOLEY:	LAUGHTER
HARRIET:	Or it could be that Dr. Watson was discreetly fibbing both times. I suggest that he was wounded someplace no Victorian gentleman would care to mention.
LAFCADIO:	Utter nonsense, Harriet. We all know what a man of the world the good doctor was.
HARRIET:	But perhaps he was a very *frustrated* man of the world, Lafcadio.
FOLEY:	LAUGHTER
NOAH:	At this late hour maybe we'd better end the discussion before we sully Dr. Watson's good name any further. So for now good night and remember: There's no police like Holmes!

FOLEY:	APPLAUSE / SCRAPING OF CHAIRS AGAINST FLOOR / FOOTSTEPS LEAVING ROOM IN DISTANCE
DUTCH: (slurred)	Can I go now?
LAFCADIO:	Only with my assistance, you pie-eyed private eye. Hold onto my arm and I'll hail us a cab.
SFX:	FOOTSTEPS OF THE TWO MEN
SFX:	FOOTSTEPS STOP / DOOR OPENS
AMBI:	STREET CORNER – EXTERIOR
LAFCADIO:	This fog is no joke. I can barely see you. A real pea-souper, as they say in England. It's almost as if . . .
DUTCH:	Don't say it, Figg. Don't even think it.
LAFCADIO:	Ah, a cab. Better still, two cabs. That smudge of yellow over there.
SFX:	FOOTSTEPS GO A FEW FEET / HALT

LAFCADIO:	Not the first cab, Dutch. Always take the second cab. The first may be dangerous.
DUTCH:	I've had enough of that Sherlock Holmes nonsense for one night. The first cab will do.
SFX:	TAXI DOOR CLOSING
AMBI:	TAXI CAB – INTERIOR
CAB DRIVER:	Where to, gentlemen?
LAFCADIO:	41 Half Moon Street. On a night like this, it ought to be Baker Street.
SFX:	ENGINE ROARS TO LIFE/ CAR PULLS AWAY / TRAFFIC NOISES
DUTCH:	With the windows down it's even foggy in here. You still with me, Figg?
LAFCADIO: (Chuckling)	Where would I go? But there's no fog in here.
DUTCH:	Can't see you. Getting a little drowsy.
LAFCADIO:	I shouldn't have bought you those last two drinks, Dutch . . . Dutch . . . Dutch!!! (Voice fades out.)

FADE TO BLACK

FOLEY: HORSES' HOOVES ON PAVEMENT / RAIN ON ROOF AND ROAD

AMBI: HANSOM CAB – INTERIOR

HOLMES: Watson! Watson!

DUTCH: Huh?

HOLMES: Ah, still among the living. For one horrifying moment I thought I should henceforth have to chronicle my own adventures.

DUTCH:
(British accent) What are you jabbering about? Who the hell are you? Where's Figg?

HOLMES: Steady, Watson. Steady.

DUTCH: Oh, I get it. A tall, skinny guy puffing on a pipe calls me Watson. I suppose you can only be Sherlock Holmes himself.

HOLMES: Surely this is a rather peculiar time for jesting, Watson?

DUTCH: You said it, mister. And a damned elaborate joke at that. Even for Figg. He must have drugged me to be able

	to do all this without waking me up. And a horsedrawn cab, no less! I wonder what it takes to hire one of these antiques in 1988?
HOLMES:	1988 . . . exactly one century hence. A remarkable thought.
DUTCH:	Mister, I don't know who you really are . . .
NARRATOR:	IT WAS SOMETHING I HEARD THAT MADE ME STOP . . . THE SOUND OF MY OWN VOICE. I SUDDENLY REALIZED I'D BEEN SPEAKING WITH A BRITISH ACCENT. FIGG COULDN'T HAVE ARRANGED THAT. I HAD TO BE DREAMING. OR MAYBE IT WAS AN ALCOHOL-FUELED HALLUCINATION . . . LIKE PINK ELEPHANTS.
HOLMES:	Watson, the rigors of that Vatican cameos affair must have affected you more than I'd thought. Pull yourself together, man. Your practical view of the most bizarre events will be especially welcome in this Madame Tussaud's case. We are, after all, on our way to meet murder in the Chamber of Horrors.

FADE TO BLACK

FORMAT:	THEME MUSIC STARTS AND STOPS
FOLEY:	HORSES' HOOVES STOP
AMBI:	OPEN STREET – EXTERIOR
CAB DRIVER (British accent):	Woah! 'Ere we are guv'nor.
FOLEY:	CAB DOOR OPENS / PASSENGERS CLIMB OUT
DUTCH:	Wait! I know you, driver! I saw you before, when I wasn't dreaming or crazy or whatever I am. You were driving the cab. Only it was a real twentieth century cab.
CAB DRIVER:	Perhaps, sir, it was the wrong cab.
HOLMES:	Watson, quit nattering. The Scotland Yarders are waiting for us.
SFX:	FOOTSTEPS / DOOR OPENING / FOOTSTEPS CONTINUE
AMBI:	LARGE ROOM / WAX MUSEUM – INSIDE
NARRATOR:	IT WAS EERIE IN THE WAX MUSEUM THAT NIGHT, WITH THE STATUES LIT ONLY BY

	GASLIGHT. AS WE WALKED, HOLMES DELIVERED A RUNNING COMMENTARY ON THE WAX FIGURES AS IF THEY WERE OLD PALS.
HOLMES:	Ah, there's Marwood, executioner to Her Majesty. Put the rope around half the murderers you see here, Watson. And there's my old friend Charlie Peace, the notorious Banner-Cross assassin and Blackheath burglar.
JONES:	Mr. Holmes! Over here!
SFX:	FOOTSTEPS STOP
HOLMES:	Our rogues' gallery is complete, Watson. Surely you remember Athelney Jones of Scotland Yard?
DUTCH:	As well as I remember . . . anything in London.
NARRATOR:	JONES WAS A PORTLY MAN IN A GREY SUIT, WITH A RED FACE AND TINY EYES ALMOST LOST IN A SET OF PUDGY CHEEKS.
JONES:	I sent for you, Mr. Holmes, because I know you love all that is out of the ordinary.

HOLMES:	As indeed this is.
NARRATOR:	JONES STOOD BESIDE A GHASTLY TABLEAU IN WAX . . . THE FIGURE OF A CRAZED-LOOKING MAN WITH A SCRAGGLY BEARD WIELDING AN AXE. AT THIS GEEK'S FEET LAY A MALE BODY, ABOUT A YARD AWAY FROM A HEAD. EVEN IN THE GLOW OF A GAS LAMP THE HEAD WAS OBVIOUSLY WAX, SHINY AND LIFELESS. THE BODY WAS ALSO LIFELESS, BUT ALL TOO REAL . . . ITS HEADLESS NECK RAGGED AND BLEEDING.
HOLMES:	Who found the body, inspector?
JONES:	This gentleman . . . Mr. Sidney Dill, guard and sometime tour leader.
SIDNEY:	It 'appened like this, guv'nor. I was makin' me presentation to a group of folk from the Salvation Army . . .
X-FADE TO:	
AMBI:	LARGE ROOM / WAX MUSEUM – INTERIOR
FOLEY:	PARADE OF FEET / MURMUR OF VOICES

SIDNEY: Now, lydies and gentleman, Madem Tussaud's is proud to present the latest terrifyin' addition to the Chamber of 'Orrors. This 'ere is Ormond Struthers, the famous Grosvenor Square Ghoul . . . 'im what chopped the 'eads off 'is victims. 'Ad 'imself a regular noggin collection, 'e did.

MALE VOICE: Cor, don't it look real!

SIDNEY: A bit *too* lifelike for some, I shouldn't wonder. Not too close, lydies.

FEMALE VOICE: Even the blood, the way it's dripping off the neck, it seems –

SFX: SCREAM

FADE TO BLACK

SIDNEY: Good thing them folks was the last of the dye. 'Twas already 'alf an hour past closing time.

HOLMES: Which gave the killer adequate time to carry out his bloody work before you came on the scene. Who was the victim, Jones?

JONES: We don't know, Mr. Holmes. He has no head, you see. None but the wax. And no identification. The victim is wearing the clothing of the wax figure he replaced.

HOLMES: What happened to the waxwork body, Inspector?

JONES: Still looking for it, Mr. Holmes.

HOLMES: Hmm. How did the murderer get it? How did he get out? And who was the victim? Those are the great questions.

DUTCH: Aren't you forgetting the little matter of the killer's identity?

JONES: No mystery about that, doctor.

HOLMES: Did I neglect to mention, Watson, that Ormond Struthers was found missing from his cell this morning? The Grosvenor Square Ghoul is on the loose tonight.

FORMAT: THEME MUSIC BEGINS AND ENDS

NARRATOR: SHERLOCK HOLMES WENT TO WORK. HE THREW HIMSELF ON THE FLOOR AND BEGAN A MINUTE EXAMINATION OF THE BODY WITH A SMALL MAGNIFYING GLASS THAT LOOKED LIKE

	THE PRIZE FROM A BOX OF CRACKER JACKS.
DUTCH:	What the hell are you doing?
HOLMES:	Gathering data, of course. One cannot deduce without it. But other than the quite obvious facts that the victim was something less than middle aged and comfortably middle class, I have learned little.
DUTCH:	Middle class? Where do you get that?
HOLMES:	What you lack in perspicacity, Watson, you make up for in consistency. How many times must I tell you to look at the hands? Surely these are not the hands of a manual laborer?
DUTCH:	Hands, huh? Hey, what about fingerprints?
HOLMES:	You mock me, Watson, but mark my words: Someday those little whirls and loops will be classified and catalogued and filed away in great depositories so that they will indeed be useful for identifying unknown persons and solving crimes.
JONES:	

(Chuckling)	You and your theories, Mr. Holmes! Now what are you doing down there on the floor again?
HOLMES:	Reading the footmarks in the dust. Shine your lamp over in that corner, Jones. Aha, I thought as much! Those marks are fresh and they don't match your shoes, Dill, or the victim's. They lead . . . right to this almost invisible door – and it's locked!
SIDNEY:	That's a storage closet. I can get the key from the manager.
JONES:	Go with him, Raven. Don't let him out of your sight.
RAVEN:	Right, sir.
FOLEY:	FOOTSTEPS DEPART / FOOTSTEPS COME TOWARD MICROPHONE / MILD COLLISION OF BODIES WITH AN "OOMPH" / FOOTSTEPS CONTINUE IN THEIR SEPARATE DIRECTION UNTIL FARTHER FADES OUT AND NEARER STOPS
MESSENGER:	Message here for Inspector Jones.
JONES:	That's me.

SFX:	FOOTSTEPS LEAVE / FADE OUT
SFX:	ENVELOPE TORN OPEN
JONES:	Damn! The Ghoul was seen near Whitechapel this evening, curse his evil soul!
SFX:	PAPER BEING CRUMPLED
JONES:	At this rate he'll be in Glasgow or Londonderry by morning!
SFX:	FOOTSTEPS APPROACH / STOP
JONES:	Ah, Mr. Dill. That didn't take long.
RAVEN:	Went straight to Mr. Joseph Tussaud himelf. (*Sotto voce*) Didn't try to run for it.
HOLMES:	Permit me to take that key.
SFX:	KEY TURNING IN LOCK / DOOR OPENING
NARRATOR:	WHAT DID I THINK WE'D FIND IN THERE . . . THE MISSING HEAD? SOMETHING GRIZZLY LIKE THAT, I GUESS. CERTAINLY NOT . . .

JONES: A bowler hat and a tweed suit wadded up behind a bucket! What's the meaning of that?

HOLMES: The suit had to be somewhere. The poor fellow who lost his head is clothed courtesy of Madame Tussaud's at the moment. I'm quite sure he didn't come in here naked, so the Ghoul must have done something with his clothing. But why change clothes at all?

SIDNEY:
(Horrified) I could swear them's the very clothes what Mr. McQuaid wore today.

JONES: And who might that be?

SIDNEY: Mr. Arthur McQuaid, sir, one of the artists . . . them what makes the wax figures. In fact, Mr. McQuaid did the Grosvenor Square Ghoul here hisself.

JONES: And I'd say the Ghoul did for him in return!

FORMAT: THEME MUSIC BEGINS AND ENDS

SFX: FOOTSTEPS WALKING DOWN EMPTY CORRIDOR

AMBI:	CORRIDOR / OPEN – INTERIOR
DUTCH:	I don't mind telling anyone I'm glad to be getting out of this place. Chamber of Horrors is an understatement.
SIDNEY:	And many's the lydy that will be weeping tomorrow from the 'orror of this night. Mr. McQuaid was quite the lydies man.
JONES:	Bachelor, was he?
SIDNEY:	Er, no sir.
JONES:	Oh. I see. Then I shall have to take the sad news to his wife. At least your part in this affair is quickly done, Mr. Holmes. We know the killer and the victim. The Yard can take it from here.
HOLMES: (Musing)	I wonder.

FADE TO BLACK

AMBI:	APARTMENT / CLOSE – INTERIOR
FOLEY:	SCRATCHING ON VIOLIN

DUTCH: Must you make that damned racket, Holmes?

NARRATOR: EVEN AS I SAID IT, I KNEW I WAS BEING UNFAIR. AFTER ALL, IT WAS MY DELUSION. IF HOLMES WAS NO VIOLIN VIRTUOSO, I COULD ONLY BLAME MYSELF.

HOLMES: Racket, Watson? Your vocabulary continues to deteriorate. You've been reading those penny dreadfuls from America again.

DUTCH: Don't change the subject. You've been scratching away on that thing all morning. I don't know why you're in such a dark mood.

HOLMES: Something's wrong, Watson. That little scene at Madame Tussaud's last night was too easy. Even the Scotland Yarders would have found McQuaid's clothes in a few hours at most.

DUTCH: But the Grosvenor Square Ghoul is a madman. He wasn't trying to hide the clothes; he was just sticking them out of the way after he set up that tableaux.

HOLMES: Then why lock the door? And where did the Ghoul get the key?

DUTCH:	From his victim, Arthur McQuaid. He found it as he was going through McQuaid's pockets. As to *why* he locked the closet, you might as well ask why he collects heads. I repeat, he's a madman.
HOLMES:	You have all the answers this morning, Watson. That alone gives me pause. Where was I? Oh, yes.
FOLEY:	SCRATCHING ON VIOLIN
SFX:	DOOR OPENS
MRS. HUDSON	Sorry to disturb you, Mr Holmes, but there's a young lady to see you. Name's Lydia Drew. Insists it's quite urgent. Something about the Grosvenor Square Ghoul.
HOLMES:	Hmm. The Ghoul again, Watson. Send her in, Mrs. Hudson.
NARRATOR:	LYDIA DREW WAS SMALL AND CHINA-DOLL DELICATE, NOT AT ALL LIKE MY GIRLFRIEND, MONA BANYON. BUT I DIDN'T LIKE HER ANY THE LESS FOR THAT.
LYDIA:	Thank you for seeing me, Mr. Holmes. You once restored a certain lost property in a discreet manner

for a close friend of mine, a Miss Teal. But of course you know nothing of me.

HOLMES: Only that you are a milliner and greatly concerned about your fiancé, whose initials are H.M.

LYDIA: Then Miss Teal –

HOLMES: Has not spoken with me in two years. You told me these things yourself by your appearance. The tiny bits of felt and glue that have attached themselves to your dress attest to your employment. But if you were not greatly upset, you would have cleaned them off before leaving your shop. You didn't even wear a hat . . . abnormal behavior indeed for a milliner. Your distress is unmistakable.

LYDIA: And my fiancé?

HOLMES: That charming locket around your neck is inscribed "To L.D. from H.M." Inasmuch as you are wearing an engagement ring, it would be peculiar indeed if the locket and the ring did not come from the same source. Mr. H.M. must be your fiancé. He did not, however, join you in this visit to Baker Street. The inference is clear that he is in some way the reason for your visit . . . and the source of your distress.

LYDIA: You are right on every point, Mr. Holmes. It is quite wonderful.

DUTCH: Really, it is childishly simple.

HOLMES: It always is, Watson . . . once I have explained it. But about your fiancé, Miss Drew?

LYDIA: His name is Henry Milburne. He is a minor clerk in an unimportant government office in Whitehall, but with strong prospects for advancement.

HOLME: Whitehall! This begins to sound like brother Mycroft's department. Pray continue.

LYDIA: Mr. Milburne and I are but newly engaged. He was to meet me at my parents' home last evening in Kensington for a small celebration in honor of the occasion. He never arrived, gentlemen. My father, who dislikes Henry, has seized upon this mysterious behavior as a sign of moral weakness. I am quite convinced there is some darker explanation.

DUTCH: Maybe there was an emergency at his office – a secret affair of state he couldn't talk about even to you.

LYDIA: But Henry told me yesterday he was going to take a holiday from the office. And I visited his landlady this morning. She said he wasn't in his apartment all evening.

HOLMES: How long have you known Mr. Milburne?

LYDIA: A little more than four months.

HOLMES: Not long, then. Affairs of the heart are Dr. Watson's department, Miss Drew, not mine. Still, I would make bold to suggest . . .

LYDIA: That something in Mr. Milburne's past has come back to claim him? Mr. Holmes, I am a mature woman living in almost the last decade of the nineteenth century. I assure you I made it my business to learn about Henry's past. There is nothing there to fear.

HOLMES: That is a delusion peculiar to young women of the modern era . . . usually cured by marriage or misadventure.

DUTCH: Holmes, you are being quite rude!

NARRATOR:	AFTER ALL, I THOUGHT, HE WAS A DELUSION HIMSELF.
LYDIA:	Actually, I appreciate your candor, Mr. Holmes. But I would value even more your talents as a detective. I am much afraid that Henry has met with foul play at the hands of the Grosvenor Square Ghoul.
HOLMES:	It is only natural that such a terrifying possibility should cloud your thoughts. The Ghoul is much the delight of the sensationalist press just now.
LYDIA:	It is more than that, Mr. Holmes. I know that Henry was planning to be in the area where the Ghoul carried out his latest horror. He told me he was going to spend the day at Madame Tussaud's!

FADE TO BLACK

FORMAT:	THEME MUSIC STARTS AND STOPS
DUTCH:	Holmes, you really are impossible! The air in here is almost unbreathable. You've been puffing on that wretched pipe for hours!

HOLMES: Only because I am a dolt this afternoon, Watson. This isn't a true three-pipe problem. The cases of Van Kirk at the Hague in '68 and Parks in Cincinnati, Ohio last year should have suggested themselves immediately. It is not happy news we must convey to our client.

DUTCH: Miss Drew? I thought you were still stewing over that Chamber of Horrors business. Surely there's no mystery about what happened to Miss Drew's fiancé. The fool did a bunk, though I can't imagine why.

HOLMES: No, Watson. I assure you, it is through no fault of Mr. Milburne's that Miss Drew will never see him again. The great question is what happens to . . . Great Scott, Watson! It will have to be done today and it is almost closing time now. We haven't a moment to lose. Grab your service revolver!

DUTCH: Revolver? Now that's the kind of detective work I can understand. But where are we going?

HOLMES: Why, to Madame Tussaud's, of course. To the Chamber of Horrors!

FADE TO BLACK

AMBI:	ROOM / OPEN – INTERIOR
SFX:	DOUBLE FOOSTEPS / SLOW
NARRATOR:	THE CHAMBER OF HORRORS WAS CREEPY ENOUGH WHEN IT WAS FULL OF COPS AND THE LAMPS ON THE WALLS WERE LIT. AT NIGHT, WITH JUST HOLMES AND ME WALKING DOWN EMPTY CORRIDORS HOLDING LANTERNS BEFORE US, IT WAS ENOUGH TO GIVE A STRONG MAN THE WILLIES. ONE BY ONE OUR LANTERNS ILLUMINATED THE MOST GRUESOME COLLECTION OF KILLERS EVER ASSEMBLED, THEIR SHADOWS DANCING CRAZILY IN THE FLICKERING FLAMES. WE WALKED PAST THE WAXWORK STATUES OF MARY ANN COTTON, POISONER OF HUSBANDS AND CHILDREN . . . BURKE AND HARE, SUFFOCATORS OF STRANGERS . . .
SFX:	FOOSTEPS HALT
HOLMES:	And so we come to Ormond Struthers. The great mystery about the first four bodies found in the immediate neighborhood of

Grosvenor Square was what had happened to their heads. You will recall that when Struthers was caught but a moment too late to save his fifth victim, the answer became clear. He had the first four heads displayed on a shelf in his bedroom . . . a rather long shelf.

DUTCH:	It looks just like we left it, except that there's no victim. I guess they never found the waxwork body.
HOLMES:	Or the real head. Watson, where would you go in a wax museum to dispose of an object the size of a man's head?
DUTCH: (Slowly)	Well . . . I guess the best thing would be to throw it in with the wax.
HOLMES:	Exactly! Once again you excel even yourself, Watson. There has to be a room in this building where wax is melted town to fashion the statues. And that's where we'll find our villain.
DUTCH:	But how do we find that room?
HOLMES:	Try every door if we have to. Come on!

FORMAT:	THEME MUSIC STARTS AND STOPS
SFX:	DOOR OPENS WITH A CREAK
AMBI:	ROOM / CLOSE – INTERIOR
DUTCH:	This is finally it, Holmes!
HOLMES:	And there's our man by that vat of boiling water.
DUTCH:	But that's not the Ghoul!
HOLMES:	Of course not, Watson. Struthers is probably halfway to Ballarat by now. That's Arthur McQuaid.
DUTCH:	McQuaid!
HOLMES:	And the gruesome sphere in his hands is his victim's head. He's going to drop it into the vat. (Shouting) Stop where you are, McQuaid, or Watson will shoot!
McQUAID:	So you saw through my little deception, Holmes. It is the famous Mr. Sherlock Holmes, isn't it? Don't come any closer or I'll drop the head. Then where will your evidence be? You won't even be able to prove who it was. By the way, who *was* the unfortunate fellow?

HOLMES: An inoffensive government clerk named Henry Milburne. You lured him away from the other patrons and killed him, didn't you?

McQUAID: He was lingering in the Chamber of Horrors after hours. A man just about my size and general shape. I promised to show him how the Grosvenor Square Ghoul claimed his victims. No man ever kept a promise better.

DUTCH: But why did you do it? You murdered a complete stranger.

McQUAID: You would prefer that I had killed a friend? Unfortunately for this Milburne fellow, I was in a spot of woman trouble. Arthur McQuaid had to die so that I could resurface somewhere else under a new identity. I needed a body that could pass for me without the head. Normally, a body without a head would be suspect . . .

HOLMES: But not if you could blame it on the Grosvenor Square Ghoul, who collected heads.

McQUAID: Exactly. The Ghoul's escape was a fortunate occurrence for me.

DUTCH:	And you hid your clothes where they would be found and point to you as the victim.
McQUAID:	But not too easily found. That might have been suspicious.
HOLMES:	Actually, it was rather the reverse. Locking the door didn't seem the action of a madman. Meanwhile, you managed to hide in this building, successfully evading the diligent searches of Scotland Yard's finest.
McQUAID:	I helped design this building. I know nooks and crannies that even Mr. Tussaud couldn't find.
HOLMES:	But hiding was only a temporary measure. You had to get out of London . . . accompanied by a female companion, no doubt. And before you did, you had to dispose of Henry Milburne's head.
McQUAID:	Quite so. Unfortunately, it is a secret no longer. Thus, I have no further use of this head. *Here!*
HOLMES: (Excitedly)	Watson, look out!
SFX:	GUNSHOT / THUD

HOLMES:	You missed, Watson. Careful, he has a gun of his own! And he's aiming at you!
SFX:	GUNSHOT / CRY OF SURPRISE AND PAIN
HOLMES:	You're hit, Watson! Are you all right? For God's sake, man, say that you are all right!
DUTCH: (Weakly)	It's real, Holmes. It's all real. At least, the pain is real. I'm not crazy after all. I'm not crazy!
HOLMES: (Frantic)	Watson! Watson!

FADE TO BLACK

APARTMENT / CLOSE – INTERIOR

MONA:	Dutch! Dutch!
DUTCH:	I'm not crazy!
MONA:	You sure could have fooled me.
DUTCH:	Mona, you're here!
MONA:	I've been here, Tarzan. I don't know where you've been.

DUTCH:	I think I've been . . . in another world, of sorts.
MONA:	That I believe. You haven't made any sense since last night. And just now you blacked out altogether for a few seconds. I've been really worried.
DUTCH:	What day is it, then?
MONA:	Sunday.
DUTCH:	Sunday and it's dark out. So I've been gone about twenty-four hours.
MONA:	I'd call it gone, all right. Are you finally finished with that corny Dr. Watson gag?
DUTCH:	Watson? I've been . . . acting like Watson?
MONA:	It drove me nuts half the time. On the other hand, you were kinda sweet. A perfect gentleman . . . in everything.
DUTCH: (As if to self)	I was so caught up in what I was doing I didn't even stop to think what must have happened to Watson . . . Believe me, Mona, I'm glad to see you. But what are you doing here in my apartment?

MONA: That friend of yours with the funny name, the old guy. He called me up last night and told me you were acting real strange. Boy, was he ever right!

DUTCH: Figg! I've got to tell him about this. He and his goofy friends were right: Sherlock Homes *was* the greatest detective of them all.

FADE TO BLACK

NARRATOR: BUT IT WAS MORE THAN A WEEK LATER BEFORE I HAD A CHANCE TO CATCH UP WITH LAFCADIO FIGG AND TELL HIM THE WHOLE INCREDIBLE STORY.

FOLEY BAR SOUNDS – GLASSES /VOICES / LAUGHTER IN BACKGROUND

AMBI: BAR / CLOSE – INTERIOR

DUTCH: . . . And then I realized that Holmes had solved the Devereaux case for me, too. You remember Harry Devereaux, the guy who died in that arson fire? Only he didn't. I tracked him down in Hilton Head, living under another name with a babe half his age. He'd killed somebody else in his place, just like McQuaid. Incredible, huh?

LAFCADIO: Quite. I don't mind telling you, Dutch, that I was concerned about your mental condition that night. And seeing you now . . . I still am. First you insist you're Dr. Watson, now you claim to have actually walked with Sherlock Holmes – a man who never lived.

DUTCH: Not in this reality, he didn't. But I think I must have somehow crossed a bridge between what we call reality and what we call fantasy. A bridge into another world or dimension or universe . . . call it whatever you want. A place where Sherlock Holmes is real and – who knows? – maybe Lafcadio Figg and Dutch Reid are fictional characters. Don't smile at me, Figg. Can you prove I'm wrong? Can you prove I didn't spend the most amazing twenty-four hours of my life in the company of Sherlock Holmes of Baker Street?

LAFCADIO: How can . . . Yes, I can, by thunder! Dr. Watson was supposed to have been alive at least as late as 1917. That was nearly thirty years after you say he was shot at Madame Tussaud's wax museum. How do you explain that?

DUTCH:	Very simply. That shot was damned painful, Figg, but it wasn't fatal. The bullet went into my . . . I mean, Dr. Waton's . . . left leg. Don't you get it, Figg. I've solved the famous problem of Dr. Watson's second wound!
HOST:	INTO ANOTHER WORLD . . . AND BACK AGAIN. BUT IN A SENSE, IT WAS A DIFFERENT DUTCH REID WHO RETURNED . . . ONE WHO WILL NEVER AGAIN BE SO CERTAIN THAT HE KNOWS THE DIFFERENCE BETWEEN WHAT IS REAL . . AND WHAT IS NOT.

THE ADVENTURE OF THE SPECKLED BAND

Dimension Radio was a project of a non-profit group called Radio Repertory Co. The president of RRC was Jon C. Hughes, who had been a journalism teacher of mine years before at the University of Cincinnati. After the Dimension Theater plays were broadcast over NPR, Jon's group conceived another idea: a series of radio adaptations of classic literature. By the end of 1992 they had funding from the Ohio Arts Council to pay for scripts and I signed a contract to produce a script for "The Adventure of the Speckled Band." In reality, by then the script was already written and had been performed. The dramatic pedigree of this particular Sherlock Holmes story is especially long. Sir Arthur Conan Doyle himself wrote the first play version. There was also a movie with Raymond Massey as Sherlock Holmes, a radio play starring Basil Rathbone, and, of course, the Jeremy Brett version from Granada Television. I consulted all of these efforts, as well as the original story, in crafting my own radio play. Jon Hughes must have been reasonably pleased with the result – he sent me an honorarium. Unfortunately, production funding never materialized and the series didn't get off the ground. My play was performed before the Tankerville Club, however, on May 25, 1990. The actors, drawn from the club membership, were (in order of appearance) Bob Plummer as the host, Barbara Herbert as Julia Stoner, Ann Andriacco as Helen Stoner, Dan Andriacco (by default!) as Sherlock Holmes, Ed Lear as Dr. Watson, and Brian Schilling as Dr. Grimesby Roylott. R.J. Senter made the most of this cast as director. Carolyn Senter provided wonderful sound effects.

FORMAT: THEME MUSIC BEGINS AND ENDS

HOST (Underscore Theme Music): Welcome to the Tankerville Players' Production of Sir Arthur Conan Doyle's "The Adventure of the Speckled Band," adapted by Daniel M. Andriacco and directed by R.J. Senter. Sherlock Holmes was created by Sir Arthur Conan Doyle and appears in stories and novels by him. Grateful acknowledgement is made to Dame Jean Conan Doyle for permission to use the Sherlock Holmes characters in this production.

FADE TO BLACK

AMBI: BEDROOM – INTERIOR

FOLEY: MUFFLED WIND HOWLING OUTSIDE / RAIN BEATING AGAINST WINDOW PANES

JULIA: This reminds me of when we were little girls in India, Helen – just the two of us, sitting in your room, talking into the night.

HELEN:	Quite so. This is probably one of the last chats we shall have before you become Mr. Scott Wilson.
JULIA:	Oh, Helen, I can still scarcely believe it. Living in this desolate house, I thought that I should never make a suitable match.
HELEN:	But you have indeed. Mr. Wilson seems such a kind and generous man.
JULIA:	Oh, he is! I only wish that you could share my happiness.
HELEN:	But I do, dear sister! I assure you that I feel your good fortune as if it were my own. And yet . . . I sense that something is troubling you. What is it, Julia?
JULIA:	Oh, nothing really, only a bit of a puzzle. Tell me, Helen, have you ever heard the sound of a whistle in the dead of night?
HELEN:	Why, no, never. Why do you ask?
JULIA:	During the last three nights, about three in the morning, I have been awakened by a low, clear whistle. I cannot tell where it is coming from, be it the next room or the lawn.

HELEN:	It must be those wretched gypsies that our stepfather allows to camp on the property.
JULIA:	Very likely. And yet, if the sound were on the lawn, I wonder that you did not hear it also.
HELEN:	But you know I sleep more heavily than you do.
JULIA:	No doubt that explains it. Well, it is getting quite late and I should be getting back to my own room.
HELEN:	Don't forget to lock your door.
JULIA:	So long as I live in a household where a cheetah and a baboon roam at will, I assure you that is an unnecessary reminder! Good night, dear sister.
HELEN:	Good night, Julia.
SFX:	FOOTSTEPS GOING AWAY
X-FADE TO:	
FOLEY:	LOUDER WIND AND RAIN
SFX:	WOMAN'S SCREAM
HELEN: (To herself)	Julia!

SFX:	DOOR OPENS/ LOW WHISTLE / LOUD CLANGING OF METAL / RAPID FOOTSTEPS / POUNDING ON DOOR
HELEN: (Shouting)	 Julia! What's wrong? What's happening?
SFX:	DOOR OPENS
JULIA: (Shrieking)	 Oh, my God! Helen! It was the band! The speckled band!
SFX:	THUD OF BODY FALLING TO FLOOR
FORMAT:	THEME MUSIC BEGINS AND ENDS
HOST	(Underscore Theme Music.): WHAT DOES A DETECTIVE LOOK LIKE? LIKE SHERLOCK HOLMES, OF COURSE! MORE THAN ONE HUNDRED YEARS AFTER HIS FIRST APPEARANCE IN PRINT, HOLMES REMAINS THE VERY PROTOTYPE OF THE UNOFFICIAL SLEUTH: BRILLIANT, ECCENTRIC, SUPREMELY SELF-CONFIDENT. HIS FAME AND

POPULARITY TRANSCEND ALL BOUNDARIES OF TIME, NATION, AND LANGUAGE. EQUALLY FAMOUS IS HIS FAITHFUL WATSON, DESCRIBED BY HOLMES AS "THE ONE FIXED POINT IN A CHANGING AGE." TOGETHER THEY APPEAR IN NINE UNFORGETTABLE BOOKS BY SIR ARTHUR CONAN DOYLE. OF THE FIFTH-SIX SHORT STORIES, AMONG THE MOST DRAMATIC IS OUR PRESENT CASE,"THE ADVENTURE OF THE SPECKCLED BAND." IT BEGINS IN APRIL 1883 IN DR. WATSON'S BEDROOM AT 221 B BAKER STREET.

X-FADE TO:

AMBI: BEDROOM – INTERIOR

HOLMES: Watson! Watson!

WATSON: Eh? Holmes! What the devil . . .

HOLMES: Very sorry to wake you at this early hour, Watson, but it's the common lot this morning. Mrs. Hudson was roused out of her sleep, she retorted upon me, and I upon you.

WATSON:

(Concerned)	What is it, then – a fire?
HOLMES:	No, a client. It seems that a young lady has arrived in a considerable state of excitement and insists upon seeing me. Should this prove to be an interesting case, I am sure you would wish to follow it from the outset.
WATSON:	My dear fellow, I would not miss it for anything.
X-FADE TO:	
NARRATOR: (WATSON)	THE WOMAN WHO AWAITED DOWNSTAIRS IN OUR SITTING ROOM WAS INDEED IN A PITIABLE STATE OF EXCITEMENT. RESTLESS, FREIGHTENED EYES LIKE THOSE OF SOME HAUNTED ANIMAL PEERED OUT OF A FACE ALL DRAWN AND ASHEN. HER FEATURES WERE THOSE OF A WOMAN OF THIRTY, BUT HER HAIR WAS SHOT WITH GRAY.
AMBI:	SITTING ROOM – INTERIOR
SFX:	CRACKLING FIRE

HOLMES:	Good morning, madam. I am Sherlock Holmes. This is my close friend and associate, Dr. Watson. Pray draw yourself up to the fire, for I see that you are shivering.
HELEN:	It is not the cold which makes me shiver, Mr. Holmes. It is fear. It is terror.
HOLMES:	You must not fear, madam. We shall soon set matters aright, I have no doubt. You have come in by train this morning, I see.
HELEN: (Paranoid)	Who told you that?
HOLMES:	You did. The second half of a return ticket is still in the palm of your left glove. I also note that you had a good drive in a dog cart along heavy roads before you reached the station.
HELEN:	Mr. Holmes!
HOLMES:	Tut, tut. There is no mystery, my dear madam. The left arm of your jacket is splattered with fresh mud in no less than seven places. There is no vehicle save a dog cart which throws up mud in that way.
HELEN:	Whatever your reasons may be, you are perfectly correct. Oh, sir, do you

think your cleverness could throw a little light on the darkness which surrounds me? In a month or six weeks I shall be married and in control of my own finances. Then you shall not find me ungrateful.

HOLMES: My profession is its own reward. Pray tell me your story, leaving out nothing.

HELEN: Very well, then. My name is Helen Stoner and I live with my stepfather. He is the last survivor of one of the oldest Saxon families in England, the Roylotts of Stoke Moran.

HOLMES: The name is familiar to me. Watson, please hand me the "R" volume of my scrapbooks. There's a good fellow. Now then, let's see. Red-Headed League . . . Giant Rat of Sumatra . . . Ricoletti of the Club Foot and his abominable wife . . . here we are: Dr. Grimesby Roylott. Fifty-five years of age, once a distinguished surgeon, beat his butler to death in India – my, my – spent years in prison for the crime, married a wealthy widow –

HELEN: That was my mother. She died in a railway accident when my twin sister Julia and I were but eight years old. She left Dr. Roylott a considerable sum of money for our care so long as we should live with him, though of course it would go to us if we should marry.

HOLMES: There was, then, no bar to your happiness.

HELEN: None save my stepfather's horrible temper. He is the terror of the village, gentlemen, a man of immense strength and uncontrollable anger. Last week he hurled the local blacksmith over a parapet into a stream. His only friends are the gypsies he permits to camp on the estate. The villagers fear his cheetah and his baboon almost as much as they fear Dr. Roylott.

WATSON: Cheetah and baboon? My word!

HELEN: Yes, he has a passion for Indian animals. He allows them to roam the grounds. He gives them more freedom than he ever afforded my poor sister and me.

WATSON: You and your sister must be very lonely.

HELEN: My sister died two years ago, Dr. Watson, and it is of the strange circumstances surrounding her death that I wish to speak to you. It

	happened within a fortnight of the day which had been fixed for her wedding to Mr. Scott Wilson, a half-pay major of marines.
HOLMES:	Pray be precise as to details.
HELEN:	The manor house at Stoke Moran is an old ruin, crushed under a heavy mortgage and generations of dissolute heirs. Only one wing is inhabited. Our bedrooms are all on the first floor. The first is Dr. Roylott's, the second my sister's, the third mine. There is no connection between them, but they all open out into the same corridor. Do I make myself clear?
HOLMES:	Perfectly so.
HELEN:	On the fatal night, my sister was troubled by the smell of the strong Indian cigars it is Dr. Roylott's custom to smoke. She left her room and came into mine, where we spent some time chatting about her approaching wedding . . .
X-FADE TO:	
NARRATOR:	HOLMES WAS ALL ATTENTION AS HELEN STONER RELATED THE STRANGE STORY OF HER

SISTER JULIA'S DEATH: THE WHISTLE, THE CLANGING NOISE, THE POOR WOMAN'S DYING REFERENCE TO A MYSTERIOUS SPECKLED BAND.

X-FADE TO:

HELEN: Dr. Roylott poured brandy down Helen's throat and sent for medical aid from the village, but all efforts were in vain.

HOLMES: One moment. Are you quite sure about this whistle and metallic sound? Could you swear to it?

HELEN: That is what the county coroner asked me at the inquiry. My honest answer must be that I believe I heard it, yet I could possibly have been deceived by the crash of the gale and the creaking of an old house.

HOLMES: And what conclusions did the coroner come to?

HELEN: The only ones possible. My evidence showed that the door had been fastened upon the inner side until Julia herself opened it. The windows were blocked by old-fashioned shutters with broad iron bars which were secured every night. The walls and the flooring were shown to be solid all around. The chimney is wide but barred up by four large staples. It is certain, therefore, that my sister was quite alone when she met her end. Besides, there were no marks of violence about her.

WATSON: What about poison?

HELEN: The doctors examined her for it, but without success.

HOLMES: What do you think that this unfortunate lady died of, then?

HELEN: Pure fear and nervous shock, I expect, though what it was that frightened her I cannot imagine.

HOLMES: Were there gypsies on the grounds that night?

HELEN: Yes, there nearly always are.

HOLMES: Ah, and what did you gather from this allusion to a band – a speckled band?

HELEN: Sometimes I have thought it was merely the wild talk of delirium, sometimes that she was referring to a band of people. Perhaps the spotted handkerchiefs which so many of the gypsies wear over their heads may have suggested the strange adjective she used.

HOLMES: Hmm. Perhaps. These are very deep waters. Pray continue your narrative.

HELEN: I have been lonelier than ever these past two years. However, a month ago I became engaged to Mr. Percy Armitage, a dear friend, and we are to be married in the spring. Two days ago, some repairs were started in the west wing of the building and my bedroom wall was pierced. I have had to move into the chamber in which my sister died and to sleep in her very bed.

WATSON: That cannot be pleasant for you.

HELEN: Indeed it is not. Imagine, then, my thrill of horror when last night I heard the same low whistle which had been the herald of my sister's death. I sprang up and lit the lamp, but nothing was to be seen in the room. As soon as it was daylight, I slipped out of the house, got a dog cart at the Crown Inn and drove to Leatherhead, from whence I have come by train seeking your advice.

HOLMES: You have done well to do so. There is not a moment to lose. If we were

	to come to Stoke Moran today, could we look over these rooms without your stepfather's knowledge?
HELEN:	As it happens, he spoke of coming to town today on some most important business. It is possible that he will be away all day.
HOLMES:	Excellent. You are not averse to this trip, Watson?
WATSON:	By no means.
HOLMES:	Then we shall both come.
HELEN:	My heart is lightened already. I shall return by the next train so as to be there for your coming.
HOLMES:	You will not join us for breakfast? Very well, then. Godspeed, Miss Stoner.
HELEN:	Good-bye for now, Mr. Holmes, Dr. Watson.
SFX:	DOOR OPENS / CLOSES
HOLMES:	What do you think of it all, Watson?
WATSON:	A most dark and sinister business.
HOLMES:	Dark enough and sinister enough.

WATSON: And yet it is hard to see another hand involved. By Miss Stoner's own testimony, her sister must have been alone when she met her mysterious end.

HOLMES: What, then, do you make of these nocturnal whistles, and what of the very peculiar words of the dying woman?

WATSON: I cannot think. No doubt you see it all!

HOLMES: Well, when you combine the whistles, the band of gypsies on intimate terms with Dr. Roylott, the fact that the doctor has a financial interest in preventing his step-daughter's marriage, the dying allusion to a band, and finally that metallic clang, which might have been caused by one of those metal bars on the shutters falling back into place, I think the solution to the mystery may be found along those lines.

WATSON: What, then, did the gypsies do?

HOLMES: That is not yet clear.

WATSON: I can see many objections to any such theory.

HOLMES:	So can I. It is precisely for that reason that we are going to Stoke Moran this day. I want to see whether the objections are fatal or if they may be –
SFX:	DOOR FORCED OPEN
HOLMES:	What in the name of the devil – !
ROYLOTT: (Loudly)	Which of you is Holmes?
HOLMES:	My name, sir. But you have the advantage of me.
ROYLOTT:	I am Dr. Grimesby Roylott, of Stoke Moran.
HOLMES:	A pretty place, I hear, and obviously good for the lungs. Pray take a seat.
ROYLOTT:	I will do nothing of the kind. My stepdaughter has been here. I traced her. What has she been saying to you?
HOLMES:	The first law in my profession, Doctor, is to answer no questions.
ROYLOTT:	You shall answer *me*. What has she been saying to you?

HOLMES: It is a little cold for the time of year, don't you think?

ROYLOTT:
(Louder, angrier) What has she been saying to you?

HOLMES: But I have heard that the crocuses promise well.

ROYLOTT: Ha! You put me off, do you? I have heard of you, you scoundrel. You are Holmes, the meddler!

HOLMES: Really?

ROYLOTT: Holmes, the busybody!

HOLMES: Well, well!

ROYLOTT: Holmes, the Scotland Yard Jack-in-office!

HOLMES:
(Chuckling) Your conversation is most entertaining, Doctor, but I am afraid I must end this interview. Life has its duties as well as its pleasures. Close the door when you go out, for there is a decided draught.

ROYLOTT: I will go when I have had my say. Don't you dare meddle with my affairs. I am a dangerous man to fall foul of. Do you hear me?

HOLMES:	You are quite audible, I assure you.
WATSON: (Excited)	What are you doing with that poker, Roylott?
ROYLOTT:	Showing you two that I am not a safe man to play with. I was the strongest man in India once. *(Grunts.)* There.
SFX:	POKER HURLED INTO THE FIREPLACE
ROYLOTT:	See that you keep yourself out of my grip or I'll twist you like I did that poker.
HOLMES:	I'll make a note of it.
SFX:	DOOR SLAMMING
HOLMES:	I had a presentiment that he would close the door. If he had remained I might have showed him that my grip was not so much more feeble than his own. (*Grunts.*) Like so.
WATSON:	You've straightened it out again!
HOLMES:	Still, I should be very much obliged if you would slip your revolver into your pocket for our trip to Stoke Moran, Watson. An Eley's No. 2 is an excellent argument with a

	gentleman who can twist steel pokers into knots.
X-FADE TO:	
SFX:	SPRING MORNING SOUNDS / HOOF-BEATS OF HORSES
NARRATOR:	AT WATERLOO WE WERE FORTUNATE IN CATCHING A TRAIN FOR LEATHERHEAD, WHERE WE HIRED A TRAP AT THE STATION INN AND DROVE FOUR OR FIVE MILES THROUGH THE LOVELY SURREY LANES. IT WAS A PERFECT DAY, WITH A BRIGHT SUN AND A FEW FLEECY CLOUDS IN THE HEAVENS. TO ME, AT LEAST, THERE WAS A STRANGE CONTRAST BETWEEN THE SWEET PROMISE OF SPRING AND THIS SINISTER QUEST UPON WHICH WE WERE ENGAGED.
AMBI:	OUTSIDE – SPRING MORNING
HOLMES:	Look over there, Watson! That must be the ancestral home of the Roylotts. Cheerful little dwelling; quite suits its master.

WATSON: That gray stone building blotched with lichen? It hardly seems livable.

HOLMES: The family must reside in that right-hand block, where the scaffolding has been set up for repairs. See the blinds on the windows and the smoke curling from the chimney? . . . Hullo! There is Miss Stoner herself.

X-FADE TO:

NARRATOR: OUR CLIENT OF THE MORNING MET US WITH ENTHUSIASM AND DIRECTED US AROUND THE OUTSIDE OF THE OLD BUILDING.

AMBI: OUTSIDE – SPRING MORNING

HOLMES: So the room where the stone-work has been broken into used to be yours, Miss Stoner?

HELEN: Exactly so. But I am now sleeping in the middle room, next to Dr. Roylott's.

HOLMES: But there does not seem to be any pressing need for repairs at that end wall, where the scaffolding is.

HELEN: There were none. I believe that it was an excuse to move me from my room.

HOLMES: Ah! That is certainly suggestive. Now, would you have the kindness to go into your room and bar your shutters?

HELEN: Of course.

SFX: FOOTSTEPS

HOLMES: This is where we put my little notion to the test, Watson. If we can open these shutters from outside –

SFX: SHUTTERS CLANG SHUT

WATSON: They certainly *look* formidable.

SFX: KNIFE SCRAPES AGAINST THE METAL SHUTTERS

HOLMES: There isn't so much as a slit to pass this knife through to raise the bar. Let us apply the lens, then, to these hinges . . . No, they are solid iron, built firmly into the masonry. Hum! My theory certainly faces some difficulties. No one could pass through these shutters if they were bolted. Well, we shall see if the *inside* of Miss Stoner's room throws any light on the matter.

X-FADE TO:

FORMAT: THEME MUSIC BEGINS AND ENDS

HOLMES: Where does that bell rope hanging down beside the bed communicate with, Miss Stoner?

HELEN: The housekeeper's room.

HOLMES: It looks newer than the other things.

HELEN: Yes, it was only put there a couple of years ago.

HOLMES: Your sister asked for it, I suppose?

HELEN: I don't know, but I never heard of her using it. We always got what we wanted for ourselves.

HOLMES: Curious. You'll pardon me if I just give it a . . . why, it's a dummy!

WATSON: Won't it ring?

HOLMES: It is not even attached to a wire. You can see now that it is fastened to a hook just above the little opening for the ventilator.

HELEN: How very absurd! I never noticed that before.

HOLMES: That is not the only singular point about this room. What a fool a

	builder must be to open a ventilator into another room when, with the same trouble, he might have communicated with the outside air!
HELEN:	That addition is also quite modern.
HOLMES:	Done about the same time as the bell-rope, I'll wager?
HELEN:	Oh, yes, there were several little changes carried out about that time.
HOLMES:	They seem to have been changes of a most interesting character – dummy bell-ropes and ventilators which do not ventilate. With your kind permission, Miss Stoner, we shall carry our researches into Dr. Roylott's apartment.
X-FADE TO:	
FORMAT:	THEME MUSIC BEGINS AND ENDS
HOLMES:	What's in this safe?
HELEN:	My stepfather's business papers.
HOLMES:	Oh, you have been inside, then?
HELEN:	Only once, some years ago.
HOLMES:	There isn't a cat in it, for example?

HELEN:	No, of course not. What a strange idea!
HOLMES:	Why, then, the saucer of milk on top of the safe?
HELEN:	I don't know, but we don't keep a cat. Just the baboon and the cheetah I told you about. My stepfather had them sent from India.
HOLMES:	Ah, yes, of course. Well, a cheetah is just a big cat, and yet a small saucer of milk does not go very far in satisfying its wants, I daresay. Now here's something else interesting. What do you make of it, Watson?
WATSON:	It's a common enough dog leash. But I don't know why it should be tied into a loop like that.
HOLMES:	That is not quite so common, eh? I think that I have seen enough now, Miss Stoner. It is essential that you should absolutely follow my advice in every respect.
HELEN:	I shall most certainly do so.
HOLMES:	Very good. Your life may depend upon it. I believe that is the village inn over there?

HELEN: Yes, that is the Crown.

HOLMES: Your windows would be visible from there?

HELEN: Certainly.

HOLMES: Miss Stoner, you must confine yourself to your room, on pretense of a headache, when your stepfather comes back from London. Then when you hear him retire for the night, you must open the shutters of your window, undo the hasp, put your lamp there as a signal to us, and then withdraw quietly into the room which you used to occupy. The rest you will leave in our hands.

HELEN: But what will you do?

HOLMES: We shall spend the night in your room, and we shall investigate the cause of this noise which has disturbed you.

HELEN: I believe, Mr. Holmes, that you have already made up your mind. For pity's sake, tell me: What was the cause of my sister's death?

HOLMES: I should prefer to have clearer proofs before I speak.

HELEN:	You can at least tell me whether my own thought is correct, that she died of some sudden fright.
HOLMES:	No, Miss Stoner, I do not think so. I think that there was probably some more tangible cause.
FADE TO BLACK	
FORMAT:	THEME MUSIC BEGINS AND ENDS
NARRATOR:	SHERLOCK HOLMES AND I HAD NO DIFFICULTY IN ENGAGING A BEDROOM AND SITTING-ROOM AT THE CROWN INN. FROM OUR WINDOW WE COULD COMMAND A VIEW OF THE AVENUE GATE, AND OF THE INHABITED WING OF STOKE MORAN MANOR HOUSE. AT DUSK WE SAW DR. GRIMESBY ROYLOTT DRIVE PAST, HIS HUGE FORM LOOMING UP BESIDE THE LITTLE FIGURE OF THE LAD WHO DROVE HIM.
AMBI:	INN ROOM – INTERIOR
HOLMES:	Do you know, Watson, I really have some scruples as to taking you

tonight. There is a distinct element of danger.

WATSON: Can I be of assistance?

HOLMES: Your presence might be invaluable.

WATSON: Then I shall certainly come. But you evidently have seen more in these rooms than was visible to me.

HOLMES: I may have *deduced* a little more, but I imagine that you saw all that I did.

WATSON: I saw nothing remarkable save the bell-rope, and what purpose that could answer I confess is more than I can imagine.

HOLMES: You saw the ventilator, too?

WATSON: Of course, but it was so small that a rat could hardly pass through.

HOLMES: I knew that we should find a ventilator before ever we came to Stoke Moran.

WATSON: My dear Holmes! How could you?

HOLMES: Recall that in Miss Stoner's statement she said that her sister could smell Dr. Roylott's cigar – that was the reason she left her room for some time on the night of her death.

	That suggested a communication between the two rooms. It could only have been a small one, or it would have been remarked upon at the coroner's inquiry. I deduced a ventilator.
WATSON:	But what harm can there be in that?
HOLMES:	Does not the curious coincidence of dates strike you? A ventilator is made, a cord is hung, and a young lady who sleeps in the nearby bed dies.
WATSON:	Yes, but . . . but I cannot see any connection.
HOLMES:	Did you observe anything peculiar about the bed in that room?
WATSON:	No, I don't believe I did.
HOLMES:	It was clamped to the floor. The lady could not move her bed. It must always be in the same relative position to the ventilator and to the rope – or so we may call it, since it was clearly never meant for a bell-pull.
WATSON: (Excited)	Holmes, I see dimly what you are hinting at. We are only just in time to

	prevent some subtle and horrible crime.
HOLMES:	Yes, Watson, when a doctor goes wrong he is the first of criminals. He has nerve and he has knowledge. This man Roylott –
WATSON:	Holmes!
HOLMES:	I see it! Miss Stoner's signal! Now our night of horror begins in earnest.
X-FADE TO:	
FORMAT:	THEME MUSIC BEGINS AND ENDS
AMBI:	EXTERIOR – SPRING NIGHT
SFX:	SOFT, SLOW FOOTSTEPS, GRUNTS
WATSON: (Near whisper)	Scaling that tumbledown wall was easy enough.
HOLMES:	You show a natural talent in the way of burglary, Watson. Climbing through Miss Stoner's window should present no –
SFX:	THUMP / ERRATIC FOOTSTEPS RUNNING

WATSON:	My, God! Did you see that, Holmes? It looked like some hideous and distorted child.
HOLMES: (Chuckling)	Charming household, is it not? That is the baboon. Quickly now, through the window.
SFX:	CLIMBING THROUGH THE WINDOW/ GRUNTS / LANDING ON THE OTHER SIDE
AMBI:	BEDROOM – INTERIOR
HOLMES: (Whispering)	Say nothing, Watson. The least sound would be fatal to our plans. And no light – he would see it through the ventilator. Sit in that chair and have your pistol at the ready. I shall sit on the side of the bed with this cane in hand.
X-FADE TO:	
NARRATOR:	HOW SHALL I EVER FORGET THAT DREADFUL VIGIL? I COULD NOT HEAR A SOUND, NOT EVEN THE DRAWING OF A BREATH, YET I KNEW THAT MY COMPANION SAT OPEN-EYED, WITHIN A FEW FEET OF ME, IN THE SAME STATE

	OF NERVOUS TENSION IN WHICH I WAS MYSELF. UNTIL –
SFX:	CRY OF A BIG CAT
WATSON: (Whispering)	Holmes!
HOLMES: (Whispering)	Shhh! It is only the cheetah.
NARRATOR:	FAR AWAY WE COULD HEAR THE DEEP TONES OF THE PARISH CLOCK, WHICH BOOMED OUT EVERY QUARTER OF AN HOUR. HOW LONG THEY SEEMED, THOSE QUARTER-HOURS. TWELVE STRUCK, AND ONE AND TWO AND FINALLY . . .
SFX:	CHURCH CLOCK STRIKES THREE IN THE DISTANCE
HOLMES: (Whispering)	Look near the ventilator, Watson.
WATSON:	A light! Roylott must be awake, then.
SFX:	LOW WHISTLE
HOLMES: (Loudly)	You see it, Watson? You see it?

SFX:	HOLMES STRIKES WITH THE CANE
WATSON:	I see nothing!
SFX:	MAN SCREAMING
WATSON:	What can it mean?
HOLMES:	It means that it is all over. Take your pistol – we are going into Roylott's room.
SFX:	FOOTSTEPS/ TWO KNOCKS ON A DOOR/ OPENING OF THE DOOR
HOLMES:	Just as I thought. Miss Stoner need no longer fear her stepfather.
WATSON:	It's ghastly, that rigid stare in his eyes. And what's that wrapped around his head? Something yellow, with brownish spots.
HOLMES:	The band, Watson, the speckled band!
WATSON:	It's moving!
HOLMES:	Be perfectly still while I take the dog leash from Roylott's hand and throw the noose – there! Now, back into the safe it goes, where the good

	doctor has been keeping it all this while.
SFX:	SAFE CLOSES
WATSON:	What on earth was that horrible creature?
HOLMES:	A swamp adder, Watson, the deadliest snake in India! Roylott died within seconds of being bitten. Violence does in truth recoil upon the violent, and the schemer falls into the pit which he digs for another.

FADE TO BLACK

SFX:	TRAIN CHUGGING
AMBI:	TRAIN COMPARTMENT – INTERIOR
WATSON:	A beastly business, Holmes. I am quite happy to be heading back to Baker Street.
HOLMES:	Ah, but in Baker Street I had come to an erroneous conclusion – which shows, my dear Watson, how dangerous it is to reason from insufficient data. The presence of the gypsies and Julia Stoner's use of the word "band" as she lay dying put me on entirely the wrong scent.

WATSON: Not for long.

HOLMES: No. I instantly reconsidered when it became clear that whatever danger threatened an occupant of the room could not come from either the window or the door. My attention was speedily drawn to the ventilator and to the bell-rope which hung down to the bed. The discovery that the bell-rope was a dummy – and that the bed was clamped to the floor – gave rise to the suspicion that the rope was there as a bridge for something passing through the hole and coming to the bed.

WATSON: A snake.

HOLMES: Yes, the idea presented itself to me immediately. When I coupled it with the knowledge that the doctor was furnished with a supply of exotic creatures from India, I felt that I was probably on the right track. The poison from such a serpent's fangs could not possibly be discovered by any chemical test. And it would be a sharp-eyed coroner, indeed, who would distinguish the two little puncture marks which would show where the poison fangs had done their work.

WATSON: The mysterious whistle in the night was Roylott recalling the snake before morning.

HOLMES: Precisely. He had trained it, probably by the use of the milk which we saw, to return to him when summoned. He would put it through the ventilator at the hour when he thought best, with the certainty that it would crawl down the rope and land on the bed. Perhaps the occupant might escape being bitten every night for a week, but sooner or later she must fall a victim. All of this was confirmed when we visited Dr. Roylott's room and saw the safe, the saucer of milk and the loop on the dog lash. The metallic clang Miss Stoner heard was undoubtedly her stepfather hastily closing the door of his safe upon its terrible occupant.

WATSON: Knowing all this, then, you were prepared to attack the snake, with the result of driving it back through the ventilator.

HOLMES:
(Jovially) And also with the result of causing it to turn upon its master on the other side. In this way I am no doubt indirectly responsible for Dr. Grimesby Roylott's death, and I

	cannot say that it is likely to weigh too heavily on my conscience.
FORMAT:	THEME MUSIC BEGINS AND ENDS
HOST:	SHERLOCK HOLMES, THE WORLD'S FIRST CONSULTING DETECTIVE, IS RETIRED NOW. HE LIVES QUIETLY UPON THE SUSSEX DOWNS, WHERE HE KEEPS BEES AND IS VISITED OCCASIONALLY BY HIS OLD FRIEND WATSON. SURELY THEY MUST REMINISCE FROM TIME TO TIME, AS OLD FRIENDS DO. AND WHEN THEIR PIPES BURN LOW, AND TALK TURNS TO DAYS GONE BY, HOW OFTEN ONE OF THEM MUST RECALL THE REMARKABLE ADVENTURE OF THE BAND . . . THE SPECKLED BAND.
FORMAT:	THEME OUT

FADE TO BLACK

Annotated Bibliography

These are by no means all of the Sherlock Holmes books that have been important to me over the years – just the ones cited in this book and the ones that I would feel guilty if I didn't mention. Most come in many editions; the editions cited are those that I own or have used.

Baring-Gould, William S., ed. *The Annotated Sherlock Holmes.* New York: C.N. Potter, 1967. Although there is now an excellent *New Annotated* by Leslie Klinger, this is the first and best-known annotated Holmes. It cites virtually all of the important Sherlockian scholarship up to its publication.

________________. *Sherlock Holmes of Baker Street.* New York: Bramhall House, 1962. The classic chronological biography of Sherlock Holmes should come with a warning to the reader: It presents as established fact much that is highly speculative – including a romance between Holmes and Irene Adler.

Doyle, A. Conan. *Adventures of Sherlock Holmes.* Illustrated by Charlie D'Andrea. Racine, Wisc.: Whitman Publishing Co., 1955. This treasured memory of my childhood is not the complete *Adventures*, but "eight popular stories by A. Conan Doyle especially selected and edited." It's not hard to find copies. I own two and have given one away.

Sir Arthur Conan Doyle. *The Complete Sherlock Holmes.* Preface by Christopher Morley. Garden City, N.Y.: Doubleday & Co. If you own only one edition of Sherlock Holmes, it should be this convenient volume. The classic Christopher Morley introduction alone is worth the price of admission.

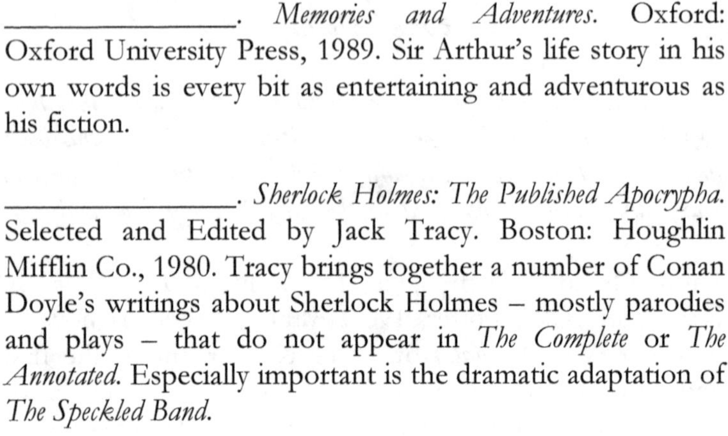

________________. *Memories and Adventures.* Oxford: Oxford University Press, 1989. Sir Arthur's life story in his own words is every bit as entertaining and adventurous as his fiction.

________________. *Sherlock Holmes: The Published Apocrypha.* Selected and Edited by Jack Tracy. Boston: Houghlin Mifflin Co., 1980. Tracy brings together a number of Conan Doyle's writings about Sherlock Holmes – mostly parodies and plays – that do not appear in *The Complete* or *The Annotated.* Especially important is the dramatic adaptation of *The Speckled Band.*

Freeman, R. Austin. *The Red Thumb Mark.* New York: Dodd, Mead & Co., 1924. Dr. Thorndyke's first case features interesting parallels to a well known Holmes adventure.

Haycraft, Howard. *The Boys' Sherlock Holmes.* New York: Harper & Row, 1961 (new and enlarged edition). In assembling this collection of three novels and six short stories, the only concession the editor made to age was the wise decision to summarize the American chapters of *A Study in Scarlet.*

Holyrod, James Edward, ed. *Seventeen Steps to 221B: A Sherlockian Collection by English Writers.* New York: Otto Penzler Books, 1994. Among many other fine essays, this compendium includes Monsignor Ronald A. Knox's seminal work, "Studies in the Literature of Sherlock Holmes."

Smith, Edgar W. *Profile by Gaslight.* New York: Simon & Schuster, 1944. Subtitled "An Irregular Reader About the Private Life of Sherlock Holmes," this is a delightful collection of some of the early essays by Holmes enthusiasts, mostly Americans.

Starrett, Vincent. *The Private Life of Sherlock Holmes.* New York: Pinnacle Books, 1975. Presented as a biography, this is really a collection of wonderful essays and, in this particular paperback edition, a brilliant pastiche by Starrett and additional material by Michael Murphy.

_______________, ed. *221B: Studies in Sherlock Holmes.* New York: Macmillan Publishing Co., 1940. Another fine collection of early essays.

Tracy, Jack. *The Encylopedia Sherlockiana.* Garden City, N.Y.: Doubleday & Co., 1977. This reference book on all things directly or indirectly Sherlockian is an indispensible resource for anyone who wants to try his or her hand at writing a Holmes pastiche.

Also from MX Publishing

Close To Holmes

A Look at the Connections Between Historical London, Sherlock Holmes and Sir Arthur Conan Doyle.

Eliminate The Impossible

An Examination of the World of Sherlock Holmes on Page and Screen.

The Norwood Author

Arthur Conan Doyle and the Norwood Years (1891 - 1894)

www.mxpublishing.com

Also From MX Publishing

In Search of Dr Watson

Wonderful biography of Dr.Watson from expert Molly Carr.

Arthur Conan Doyle, Sherlock Holmes and Devon

A Complete Tour Guide and Companion.

The Lost Stories of Sherlock Holmes

Eight more stories from the pen of John H Watson – compiled by Tony Reynolds.

www.mxpublishing.com

Also From MX Publishing

Watsons Afghan Adventure

Fascinating biography of Watson's time in Afghanistan from US Army veteran Kieran McMullen.

Shadowfall

Sherlock Holmes, ancient relics and demons and mystic characters. A supernatural Holmes pastiche.

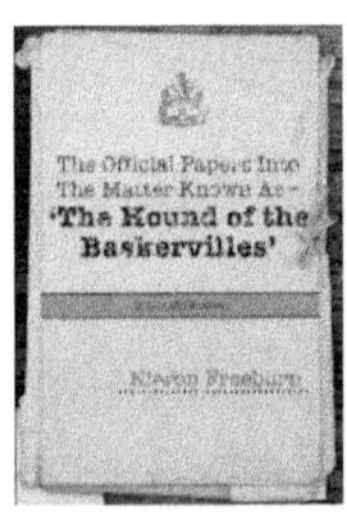

Official Papers of The Hound of The Baskervilles

Very unusual collection of the original police papers from The Hound case.

www.mxpublishing.com

Also From MX Publishing

The Sign of Fear

The first adventure of the 'female Sherlock Holmes'. A delightful fun adventure with your favourite supporting Holmes characters.

A Study in Crimson

The second adventure of the 'female Sherlock Holmes' with a host of sub-plots and new characters joining Watson and Fanshaw

The Chronology of Arthur Conan Doyle

The definitive chronology used by historians and libraries worldwide.

www.mxpublishing.com

Also From MX Publishing

Aside Arthur Conan Doyle

A collection of twenty stories from ACD's close friend Bertram Fletcher Robinson.

Bertram Fletcher Robinson

The comprehensive biography of the assistant plot producer of The Hound of The Baskervilles

Wheels of Anarchy

Reprint and introduction to Max Pemberton's thriller from 100 years ago. One of the first spy thrillers of its kind.

www.mxpublishing.com

Also From MX Publishing

Bobbles and Plum

Four playlets from PG Wodehouse 'lost' for over 100 years – found and reprinted with an excellent commentary

The World of Vanity Fair

A specialist full-colour reproduction of key articles from Bertram Fletcher Robinson containing of colour caricatures from the early 1900s.

Tras Las He huellas de Arthur Conan Doyle (in Spanish)

Un viaje ilustrado por Devon.

www.mxpublishing.com

Also From MX Publishing

The Outstanding Mysteries of Sherlock Holmes

With thirteen Homes stories and illustrations Kelly re-creates the gas-lit, fog-enshrouded world of Victorian London

Rendezvous at The Populaire

Sherlock Holmes has retired, injured from an encounter with Moriarty. He's tempted out of retirement for an epic battle with the Phantom of the opera.

www.mxpublishing.com

www.ingramcontent.com/pod-product-compliance
Lightning Source LLC
LaVergne TN
LVHW010102110826
845155LV00028B/444

* 9 7 8 1 9 0 8 2 1 8 9 2 6 *